MW01230418

Praise for Black Rain Season

"If Stephen King's best coming-of-age work took place in Florida, you'd have *Black Rain Season*. Excellent, fast-paced story featuring heartfelt characters and an exceptionally creepy killer. I loved this book and know you will too." —Sonora Taylor, award-winning author of *Little Paranoias: Stories and Without Condition*

In the Sunshine State, the weather is hot and the people are shady. Kayli Shultz's *Black Rain Season* drips with dark, southern gothic goodness in a slow burn mystery that unravels deliciously with each horrific turn of the page. — Wendy Dalrymple, author of *White Ibis* and *Parasocial*

"Viciously exciting and unrepentantly queer while hitting all the nostalgic notes, BLACK RAIN SEASON is a haunting gothic masterpiece and Scholz is a master of Southern horror." —Sirius, author of *Rising Sun Over the Devil's Nest*

"Grim, heartfelt, eerie, and hopeful. An evocative dream of Halloween." —Johnny Compton, author of *The Spite House* and *Devils Kill Devils*

"Scholz is a master at creating unforgettable villains who wrap their fingers around the throats of everyday people and refuse to let go, mutating every seemingly innocent interaction into a sinister omen. I loved every second of it." —Tiffany Meuret, author of *Flood of Posies*, *Little Bird*, and *Cataclysm*

BLACK RAIN SEASON

By Kayli Scholz

Curious Corvid
PUBLISHING

Cover Art by Matthew Revert
Formatted by Ravven White

ISBN: 978-1-959860-43-3
978-1-959860-44-0

Printed in the United States of America
Curious Corvid Publishing, LLC
PO Box 204
Geneva, OH 44041

This is a work of fiction. Unless otherwise indicated, all the names,
characters, businesses, places, events and incidents in this book are either
the product of the author's imagination or used in a fictitious manner.
Any resemblance to actual persons, living or dead, or actual events is
purely coincidental.

www.curiouscorvidpublishing.com

First Edition

Dedication

This one's for Serdar.

OCTOBER 23

I

etty Hardin heard the dead. It wasn't make-believe or a phase. It started around the time her dad, Hank, died of sudden cardiac arrest while battling long Covid. He'd been operating a forklift at the sugarcane mill and never came home. Two weeks after he died, Letty could sense him all the time, everywhere she went. It was a sound that tickled her inner ear, like a humming refrigerator, low and steady. She felt warm when he was around. But since she'd turned twelve, that humming had dwindled, and the only thing she knew for certain was her dad had been gone for two years.

Pretending she could still hear the dead made Letty feel better. Maybe if she practiced enough, it would come true.

Letty and her mother, Jane, lived in a backcountry rural town in Florida. Sugar Bends, northwest on the peninsula, population: 9,930. Sugar Bends was a dark place. Not enough sunlight shone over the tallgrass prairies, and the southern live oaks and laurel branches arched dramatically in the woods that strangled the town. The thunder always boomed louder in Sugar Bends, and the people were stranger.

The year lurched forward into the new moon of October as Sugar Bends's serial killer, the Hillbilly Hammer, was still at large. Letty's mom stocked up on pepper spray and made the executive decision that Letty was to always carry a canister. The killer could be anyone. All the leads law enforcement ran with were duds, and the town was on an indefinite curfew of 11:00 p.m. Despite the lockdown, a teenage girl was murdered on October 13, and everybody was frantic, bringing the body count to six deaths since January, and one disappearance. The FBI investigated, and local media from Hounds, the nearby rural town north of Sugar Bends, was all over it. But the dead girl barely made headlines. The same day, there had been another school shooting one county over, and Sugar Bends's killer was demoted to the back page.

Margot Henry was the latest headline. She was a popular eighteen-year-old girl nicknamed "Babes," a basketball and track star with a four-year academic scholarship to Georgia Tech, a prize unheard of in Sugar Bends. Babes Henry was bludgeoned to death with a titanium hammer. She was buried on the third Sunday of October at Barrett's Cemetery. There weren't any cameras or media in attendance, but half of the student body showed up with rafts of flowers.

Letty and her best friend, Bernie Acosta, were hell-bent on

seeing Babes's gravesite. They were twelve and couldn't help but fawn over the teenage tragedy. They were sad, too—devastated—but nothing like this had ever happened to a girl their age before in Sugar Bends. Besides, Letty thought, cemeteries were good places to talk to people you loved after they'd moved on to the permanent dark. She thought hanging out in Barrett's Cemetery might get her closer to her father again.

They hadn't known Babes Henry, not personally. She went to Earl Jones High School, and they were still at Earl Jones Middle. Now she was gone without really leaving, stuck in a weird shadow place Letty and Bernie couldn't touch. Half-departed. Gone but not forgotten. Just like Letty's dad.

They planned to leave for the cemetery when the coast was clear. After Letty's mom came home from waiting tables all day, she flipped on her table fan next to the bed. Letty knew the white noise meant her mom had gone to sleep, code for *don't bother me unless the house is on fire.* That was her signal. Letty grabbed her messenger bag and met Bernie at the end of their street on Loxahatchee Road.

Bernie held a bouquet of supermarket flowers. She'd broken her arm skateboarding and had been in a cast the last six weeks. Her frizzy black hair stopped above her shoulders,

and her eyeglass frames were too big for her naturally ruddy
face.

"Thought you said you were getting roses to put on her
grave," Letty said.

"These are roses."

"Those are carnations."

"Same shit."

"I forgot the pepper spray."

"Shoot. What if there's creeps out there?" Bernie said,
scrunching her nose. "Men lurk in those woods."

"You're carrying on," Letty said, repeating a phrase her
mother said to her often. But she was nervous too, worried
about the tall grass among the graves—a perfect hiding place
for creepy guys. She didn't want Bernie to know.

Barrett's Cemetery was a one-mile hike north, wedged along
a basin marsh across from Bethel Road, where the smell of
burning sugarcane would be replaced with rank sewage in
springtime. But this was autumn, and the flashing signs still
warned of reduced visibility from the smoke. Photocopied
flyers, brittle and almost unreadable with age, were still taped
to utility poles.

MISSING: NANCY RUSSO. SINCE 12/28/23.
LAST SEEN AT MELL'S 100% CITRUS AND
NURSERY.

Even in the dark, Letty and Bernie found their way easily. The air crackled with tension, lighting their nerve endings better than any streetlights.

"I'd feel bad if I had to pepper spray anybody," Bernie said.

"Not if they're trying to rip your pants off."

"You're messed up, Letty."

"What? *You're* messed up." Letty wished she'd brought a hair tie. She had the longest hair in their class, dishwater blond, down to the middle of her back. She was proud of its length.

"Who says shit like that? You watch too much *Game of Thrones*."

"You watch more than me!"

"Check it, look at this asshole in that car," Bernie said.

A driver, probably one of the Timber gang kids from the high school, flipped them off, bleating the horn as he pulled around a blind curve.

The girls shouted obscenities as he sped off. There was a lot of anger in Sugar Bends lately. Neighbors were shuttering windows with plank wood and not going out after dark. Some people offered to look after each other's houses while they were at work or went to the market. People feared the Hillbilly Hammer.

"That dude shouldn't even be out. It's past curfew," Letty said.

"Look who's talking."

When they arrived at the cemetery, Letty and Bernie jumped the paddock fence, stepping on dried red buckeye that hadn't survived the dog days of hurricane season. Sharp twigs, once blooming with wildflowers, scraped their legs in the wild brush. Their feet crunched leaves as they walked along rows of graves.

Sugar Bends was referred to as the "Boonies" by the folks in Hounds, Florida, because it was so far away from the rest of the world. Its economy had depended on harvesting sugarcane and lumber since the plastic factories shut down. If you didn't work in the sugar mill or the lumber yard, you were either a kid like Letty and Bernie, or you were a Boonie, working in the supermarket or diner.

Older headstones had etchings that looked ancient in comparison to the new limestone work. There was an old grave the girls always walked by, with the weathered inscription:

NOLAN PETERS CRAVEN

DECEMBER 1, 1960–JANUARY 19, 1988

That year seemed like it was so long ago it was almost

imaginary to the girls.

"We can take turns saying something to Babes," Letty said, returning her focus to Bernie. "I can feel her presence already." They'd played in the graveyard a hundred times, but this time was different; they were coming to visit a girl from their own town.

"I 'dunno, Letty, you still think you can talk to the dead? I feel like we're getting too old for playing that stuff."

Letty sighed, offended. She partly blamed Bernie's attitude on her jerk-o sixteen-year-old brother, Joe, who was always ragging on them. "I don't *think* I can, I *know* I can. It's not playing. It's business."

"Aw, don't get glum, chum. Said I was sorry."

"Nuh-uh, you didn't."

"I'm *sorry*, Letty. It's just you're gonna get your panties in a twist if you don't hear from Babes Henry."

The girls were quiet for several minutes. Bernie took out her Off! Deep Woods bug spray and wet her legs. They were used to mosquito swarms on their trips to the cemetery. Being just outside the basin marsh, mosquitos thrived in pockets of water puddled around the headstones and weeds. She passed the spray to her friend without speaking, the two of them moving in silent tandem.

Letty and Bernie met in the fourth grade, and Letty shot up a foot seemingly overnight on the first day of seventh grade. She was proud of her hair but embarrassed by her height, apple cheeks, and dimples. Bike rides and their Talking Dead Society club, where they practiced séances, were becoming less important to Bernie as she expressed disinterest in *playing* anymore.

"Hope I don't cry at her grave," Bernie said.

"I *will* cry."

The sky was filled with bright flecks of stars; it was unusual to see them this time of year, when the controlled burnings were carried out at the mill. It was hot. The heat wave hadn't broken since Labor Day. They took the long way, walking over busted cypresses and sumac bushes. They whispered about the Hillbilly Hammer, asking each other aloud if that rustling in the bushes was the killer. But Letty knew better. It was an opossum—must have been.

"Maybe you should get the pepper spray ready, just in case," Bernie said.

"I told you; I don't have it. I'd look like a psycho anyhow."

Letty and Bernie walked quietly over the flank of the hill they'd just climbed, full of weeds and croaking frogs. Bernie pulled a branch out of a leafy hedge, pointing it skyward.

"I saw the high school girls yesterday. They looked real beat up about Babes. Three of them were even crying," Bernie said.

"Hey, Bernie, you think if Babes Henry had known us, we would've been friends?"

Bernie shrugged. "Maybe. She's eighteen—was—eighteen. We're twelve."

Letty hugged the messenger bag closer to her hip, feeling a gust of warm wind. "Technicalities."

"Yeah, technicalities. You know, Letty? I miss her even though I didn't know her."

"Babes Henry sees us from Heaven."

Bernie laughed. "You believe in Heaven now?"

"What the heck's so funny about that?"

"There's no such thing."

"You don't know."

The foliage got thornier the deeper they hiked into Barrett's Cemetery. The ground dipped between burial mounds, and the girls were careful to sidestep the tiny lambs and angels that marked the graves of lost infants and unborn children. They knew the terrain; two summers ago, they played in the cemetery every weekend, making fun of the names on the headstones. On the older side of Barrett's, where not a lot of people visited anymore, a grave was marked Fran Farton—

Farton. It was a belly laugh for weeks.

Twenty yards away, a coyote feasted on an animal carcass.

"Gross," Bernie said. "Let's pick up the pace."

"Mom would have a cow if she knew we were out here, especially without the pepper spray," Letty said.

"Your mom has a cow over a lot of stuff lately."

Bernie was right. The whole town was shaken up by the Hillbilly Hammer, especially Letty's mom, who'd been a nervous wreck since the killings started. Nobody could give a description of the Hillbilly Hammer's face; he was too nimble a runner, too mechanical to leave a trace. Only his Chippewa boots were identified, and it wasn't difficult to find three-quarters of the town wearing the same boots at the mill or lumber yard.

Letty shrugged, slapping her arm where it itched from the heat. "My mom was having a cow before the Hillbilly Hammer."

Jane Hardin, Letty's mom, seemed to shrivel when she watched the news, which was on all the time in their house. She was terrified, like everybody, and just waiting for the next body to be found. The extended curfew only made it worse, turning Sugar Bends into a pressure cooker where everybody felt like something bad was about to happen.

"Shh," Bernie said, halting Letty with her good arm. "Over there, I think I see it."

Babes's headstone. There it was, newly planted. They smelled damp lime rock, the sweat of the earth.

MARGOT ANNE HENRY

BORN APRIL 2, 2006

DIED OCTOBER 13, 2024

REST IN PEACE BEAUTIFUL GIRL

The grave was surrounded by big batches of yellow peonies. Letty gently kicked at the fresh soil. Her eyes swelled with tears.

"Wow, she's really dead," Bernie said.

"It's weird."

"Yeah."

Letty felt her chest swell with the same sadness she felt when she thought about how her dad had loved her once. He'd been alive and real, and he loved her. A shiver ran from her collarbone down her spine.

"I think I feel Babes Henry, Bern. I do. I feel her here with us right now."

Bernie scrunched her face. "You know something, Let, I've been thinking. I don't really think I *feel* anything. I think the séances are just a game."

Letty closed her eyes, trying to focus on the shiver on her

skin. She pretended, imagining she could feel the humming electricity again, her father, all around her. She pretended it was Babes Henry. "No, Bernie, she's here. She's swirling all around us. It's like . . . Babes is finally free."

"Come on, Letty, quit clowning around."

Letty put her messenger bag by a tree stump. She spun in a gentle circle, ears picking up the sawing sounds of the cicadas in the nearby trees. She hoped Bernie saw just how tightly her eyes were closed, so she could comprehend the seriousness of the moment. *See, Bernie,* she wanted to say, *it wasn't a game, look, I'm spinning and hearing the dead.* This was important. More important than video games or spying on neighbors or riding bikes.

When Letty quit spinning, she glanced at Bernie, who bent down in front of the peonies.

"She's gone. Dead as a doornail. Bought the farm."

They didn't cry but they told each other they were crying. Letty rummaged through the messenger bag for a lighter and two tea candles that barely illuminated their feet.

"Your mom would have a cow at this too," Bernie said, shaking her head.

"I'd like to say a few words to the girl that was—"

"Woman."

"—*woman* that was Babes Henry."

The girls had just learned about feminism and took it seriously, correcting their peers when *girl* was used, in their opinion, disrespectfully.

"We're sorry you died."

"We want you to be at peace in Heaven." Letty glanced sharply at Bernie, who rolled her eyes. "You're dead now, so, there's no more hardship. No more high school drama. No more pain. May you . . . dream forever. You were so, so beautiful."

"*So* beautiful," Bernie said. "The most beautiful girl in the school."

"I'll miss you forever."

"I'll miss you forever, also."

The girls each threw a handful of dirt into the air, pretending it was something more spiritual than cemetery soil. Letty touched the lettering of the death date, October 13. She kissed the plastic mood ring on her index finger for good luck.

It began to rain, and a warm gust knocked out the tea candles. They trudged back to the street, taking the long way again, back over the paddock fence and sumac bushes. They kept their eyes peeled for cops, who would drag them home and put up a fuss over curfew. They got back to Loxahatchee

Road with damp hair from the heat, the canopy of trees and a flashing Reduced Visibility sign disappearing.

"Bernie, you believe me about hearing the dead and stuff, right?"

She shrugged. "Sure. Just don't get weird about it."

"I'm not weird."

Bernie playfully struck Letty in the shoulder, and she did it back. "Talking Dead Society forever—right?"

"You bet."

"Cool. See you tomorrow."

"See you, Bern."

Letty stood in front of her family's powder blue cracker house, drawing the warm night air deep into her lungs. White cement bricks raised the floors by a half-broken white trellis beneath the porch, surrounded in crabgrass. The pitched roof was half metal and half cedar, with a block chimney shrouded in moss. She quietly went inside, making sure the windows were closed and the door was locked.

A man covered in midnight shadows watched Letty from the sidewalk.

OCTOBER 24

I

Theo Shortridge scraped chunky brain matter off a scuffed loveseat. Cleaning up old muscle felt like carving sirloin. It came off in thin layers as she moved the metal scraper up and down over the furniture. The body of her client's dead spouse had been imprinted on the loveseat in the corner of the bedroom. Feces were dried into the white cushion, unsalvageable. It formed a smelly, dried lump in a mass of blood. Everything went into a Santa-red biohazard bag.

Theo turned off The Clash's "Straight to Hell." She wasn't in the mood for music. The morning news blared on the TV in the next room; the FBI hunt for the Hillbilly Hammer had been stalled, what else was new? Theo had known they'd lose the trail five months ago, when they talked of scrapping the investigation altogether. Rural Florida towns with a population of less than ten thousand weren't exactly priority to the feds.

Theo got on her knees and used a high-powered light to inspect the bedpost. She'd stripped the bed of linens, removed the mattress, and tossed the bedding into the biohazard bag, even though the dude committed suicide on the loveseat. Blood had sprayed, taking life with it. She found loose teeth on the floor. She hadn't been given permission to pull up the carpet, so disinfecting would have to suffice.

Guts and bodily tissue didn't faze Theo. Death was natural, not gross. Like snot or period blood or piss, it was a part of life. She used to think about becoming a medical examiner, counting limbs and identifying butchered, ripped off faces. She'd make more money. Or doing surgery. Surgery was different. The body parts were where they should be, anatomically speaking. There was an A, B, C approach to most of those sciences, and you had a team. Doctor, medical examiner, or crime scene technician—these professions were very different, yet very much the same. Darker sides of the same science.

Theo was in the cleanup business. She'd been hired for a job in Hounds, eight miles north of Sugar Bends. No town was absolved of human horrors. She cleaned up suicides, murders, the homes of hoarders, shooting aftermaths, and meth and Fentanyl labs. All the doozies. Sometimes the cleanups were days or weeks post-death, sometimes hours. She was all too familiar with guilty survivors, and she was now one of them, in her own way.

The worst part of her grief was the miserable feeling that she deserved it. Maybe she did.

Her wife, Nancy Russo, disappeared last winter just before New Year's, and she was almost certain the Hillbilly Hammer was responsible. One morning, Theo dropped Nancy off at the citrus and plant nursery she'd worked at for twenty years. That evening, when Theo went to pick up Nancy, nobody had seen her since she'd clocked in that morning. Her disappearance happened sometime between 7:59 a.m. and 8:25 a.m. Three weeks after that, the killings started in earnest. There was a murder, then another murder, and another.

Since Nancy disappeared, Theo had toed the vital margin between sanity and nervous breakdown. Her Zoloft prescription convinced her she had her shit together, even throughout her all- consuming grief. She missed Nancy very much, but she still had to go to work every day. She still had to survive.

Theo's braids were neatly stacked on top of her head underneath her ballooned hazmat suit, and her indigo bifocals fogged up under the respirator. She had nineteen sleeve tattoos on her arms and collarbone; inked on the fingers of her left hand was the word "JAM."

She found squiggles of blood and guts and bone tissue spurted on the ceiling. She maneuvered on a ladder to reach and scrub. Times like these, she needed a tech assistant, but the more hands-on she was, the less she thought about her own problem: Nancy was gone. When she got home from work tonight, Nancy would still be gone.

Most of the time, Theo's gig was a disinfect and scrub, but this case in Hounds was special because her client, Agatha Bigelow, had waited ten days before calling 911 while her husband's body decomposed in their two-bedroom apartment. She probably couldn't take the smell anymore, or a neighbor complained of an odor.

Clients were typically shy about how people died. Sometimes they apologized, especially with suicides or drug dens. Guilt is the same in every family.

Theo, on the other hand, enjoyed the gritty details. She told her clients that no job was too dirty; she was required to know every bit of the forensics and circumstantial evidence so she could remediate the mess effectively. She didn't feel sorry for anybody. It wasn't that she was heartless, it was just that she was desensitized to gunshots and suicides. You had to be straight-faced in this business. You needed a guard. She'd been a crime scene cleanup tech for twenty years, following in nobody's footsteps except the exhibitive tragedies of the dead and their families.

She joined Agatha Bigelow in the TV room. She removed

the respirator and her bifocals. Her white hazard pants expanded when she walked like a Jiffy Pop pan.

"You all done?" the feeble old woman asked. She gripped a walker even though she was stationed in front of the TV. Her nightgown was filthy.

The news was over. *Family Feud* began.

"Mrs. Bigelow, I'm suggesting your landlord replace the carpeting in the bedroom. You're looking at an odor problem six months down the line."

"I wish you'd called first before you showed up with all this ruckus."

Theo nodded, folding the rubber gloves into the pocket of the hazmat suit. "The bedroom is stained, meaning your husband's remains got into the rug. I'm sorry to get graphic with you, but that's reality. If the carpet's replaced, the room will be as good as new. You can give the owner my card if there's any questions."

A young man walked into the living room. He was tall and lanky with jet black hair and wore an Adidas tracksuit. "Aggie, what do you want for supper?"

"My mac and cheese."

The young man went to the kitchen, asking Theo if she wanted any.

"The landlord will look at it," Mrs. Bigelow concluded. "Call first next time."

When Theo finished, she locked the windows without telling Mrs. Bigelow. Safety was instinct at this point in Sugar Bends and Hounds: check your doors, check your windows, check the backseat, and check the goddamn linen closet.

"Again, I'm sorry for your loss."

The young man, presumably her grandson, thanked Theo.

Theo undressed in her work van, where she'd drive to the county hospital and dump the hazard materials. She dinged around on her phone, turning up her favorite Neil Young song, "Unknown Legend." She was the woman in the song, she thought, as she pulled onto northbound I-75, the pine flatwoods coming into view. She was barely hanging on by a thread, forty, with silver hair that once flew in the wind as she rode on a chrome motorcycle. She missed her wife's magic kiss. Her Triumph motorcycle was parked in the yard, covered with tarp, untouched since Nancy's disappearance.

On the way to the county hospital, Theo remembered her Xanax script was almost out and she'd need to call the doctor. Just willpower and Zoloft wouldn't cut it. God, she missed Nancy. She wanted to know Nancy was all right. Full-on love. Her cinnamon girl.

A week into Nancy's disappearance, the police informed Theo her wife's return was unlikely. The way it had happened, Theo having driven her to work, fit the criteria of a "wake up and run" case. Cheaper than a divorce, the cop said. He suggested Nancy had just taken off. No credit card withdrawals, no foul play, no evidence of infidelity or self-harm. The fact of the matter was, Theo knew Nancy wasn't dead and hadn't started her life over, either. Nancy Russo was very much alive no matter what law enforcement said.

Theo could hear the dead, everywhere, all the time. Had since she was about eleven years old. But she couldn't hear Nancy at all. So, Nancy couldn't be dead.

Nancy was missing.

Theo arrived at the hospital and checked in with the waste coordinator. It was a pallid afternoon, only a few hours until twilight. Once she was alone, dumping disposal bags of intestinal pieces and bloodied linens, the sensation of soft electricity latched onto her. In these ruthless cases, the feeling came at full charge, no warning, like floodlights turning on inside of her. She dumped the last bag into the embedded red waste overhang, her eyes scanning the back area of the hospital.

A hospital was like a million ticking clocks for her, but she rarely felt it like this, especially while on the job wearing earbuds with music playing in her ear. Near another row of industrial red garbage bins, across the hot tarmac, a coyote with the blackest eyes looked back at her.

II

Sweet Jesus, the heat. Angie Johnson stuck George Jones's *Super Hits* into the pickup's tape deck. She sang the song "He Stopped Loving Her Today" in a high pitch to her new groom, Josiah Sullivan. She had her baby on her mind, her Josiah man, though he probably had sleep on his. They'd been cooped up for nine hours in the Chevy since Morristown, Tennessee. All that wilderness they left behind. She hoped never to see it again.

Once every hundred miles, Angie asked Josiah to open the glove compartment so she could see their .32 starter pistol, safe and sound.

Angie pulled off I-75. She'd been smoking Newport's since Decatur, switched from Kools on a whim at the last gas station. Cracker houses and railroad tracks and motels with faded cola signs on the roofs came into view. Skunk fumes clung to the front grill from some stinky roadkill around Tallahassee.

"Smoking's out of style since 1999," Josiah said. "And what if we got a bun in your oven?"

"Joey, you know I gotta do something to keep on driving. My hand needs something to do."

Josiah smirked, throwing his '69 Chevron ball cap on the

dash. "I don't want our baby comin' out deaf and dumb."

Angie watched the speedometer. The last thing they needed was to get pulled over by patrol. She decided on forty in a forty-five. *Safe as houses*, she thought. They were gonna be okay.

They'd been on the run from Angie's old man, Mitch, and the whole angry First Baptist Church back home in Morristown after he'd framed them for robbing the deacon, who'd been filling in for the church secretary. Mitch had gotten them on surveillance snooping through the church secretary's unsecured safe and desk drawers, and although *they* hadn't taken anything, he'd seen an opportunity to set them up and get rid of their sinful-ass ways. Angie's dad stuffed two thousand dollars in cash into their glove compartment with the unregistered handgun. He went and shot the church secretary's husband at the state store, then called 911 to report two kids in a Chevy, fleeing the scene.

If Angie and Josiah showed their faces in Morristown again, they'd get picked up by the authorities, or, worse, Mitch.

They got married on Angie's eighteenth birthday in a chapel in Boulder City. All they had now was each other, on the run with no plan in sight except the stashed two thousand dollars and a drywall job from a friend out there near Mountain View, Arkansas. They'd crashed on the kid's sofa for a week, and

Josiah made three hundred and twenty-five dollars. After that was gone and they'd reached Montgomery, they had no choice but to use the stolen money for motels, food, and gas. It added up. Soon they'd have nothing at all.

"How long have I been driving, Joey?" She liked to tell the story, and he liked hearing it.

"How long, baby?

"Since I was eleven years old."

Angie was proud of this fact. She didn't have much in the way of a proper education, but she sure could drive. She could drive anywhere. Lately, all they talked about was where they were off to next.

"Hey, Joey, what do you think my old man's gonna do when he finds out we got hitched?"

Josiah perched his elbow over the open window. "We've been over this. He ain't gonna find out—'cuz we're gonna hole up someplace and I'm gonna work drywall. Then we go someplace else until we can afford a house."

"Maybe an apartment," Angie said.

"Apartments are for poor people, Angie. I told you this."

Angie nodded, gripping the steering wheel. How much money did a house cost? She guessed maybe fifty thousand dollars; maybe even less than that since everybody got laid off when Covid-19 came to town. You paid for that and then you had a house. If Josiah made four hundred dollars a week fixing drywall, and if she made good tips at a diner, worked hard, they'd have that house money in a few years. She'd do the math on paper later.

But her groom, her cowboy, would take care of her. They promised in front of God.

"Sorry, Joey. I won't ask again."

"It's fine." The truck, smelling of turpentine, glided over the back roads as they looked for their stop. They had enough cash to fill up the Chevy, thank you Jesus, always on good terms. Angie nodded to the wooden crucifix hanging in the rear view.

"Shit and Shinola," Josiah said. "There's a lot of cops hangin' out around Sugar Bends."

"Is that where we're at?"

"I think so. Smell that? Heavy." He coughed into his fist.

"Smokey out here."

The last place they lodged for more than a couple weeks was Broken Arrow. Before that, Tupelo. Angie really wanted to call it a night. She was sick and tired of being in the Chevy, and frankly, she could tell Josiah was getting antsy too.

Josiah liked saying, "no harm done that's harming the

white-collar man," but he was up to his knees in sins, and they hadn't been to church since their wedding day. They stole from a Walmart in Montgomery, which was called in to local law enforcement (who they lost on the interstate), and from a gas station in Knoxville. It was usually food. Nothing came easy except for George Jones on the radio.

When Angie saw the sign for Mayday Motel, she was relieved for the stop. The one-level building was straight out of 1980, with a sign advertising cable and air conditioning. There were electrical pylons in the tallgrass prairie across the road. The night manager gave them an old- fashioned key with a big green flap.

"That mongrel out there," Josiah said. He pointed across to the prairie, the horizon line a glistening sheen of fading orange. The heat was unremitting. "See the dog?"

"That's a coyote," Angie corrected.

The coyote looked hungrily at them from the road, full of a human-like malice Angie could only register as rabid. *A man's anger*, Angie thought, wondering why she thought that way at all about the animal.

"Come on inside, Joey," Angie said, opening the motel room door. "That thing's creeping me out."

But as she looked around the motel room, she realized it

wasn't much better. The walls were painted granny green except for a strip of wallpaper with ducks on a pond in the bathroom.

"Honeymoon suite," Josiah smiled.

"Nicer than the last motel with the air conditioner that dripped water all over my clean clothes," Angie said.

"And not one dirty pig pulled us over for that broken taillight." He plopped on the bed. The springs squeaked. The room smelled like generic hand soap you'd find in a pump at a rest stop. The Mayday Motel sign flickered like a half-broken headlamp through the window.

"Who cares about the taillight," Angie sighed. "I'm worried about the carburetor and transmission and the rear tires. I don't know how much farther that thing's gonna take us. We're lucky we didn't kick the bucket on the 95."

"Look, baby," Josiah said, patting the bed. "We got nowhere to go 'cuz we're out of gas, right?"

"Almost, yeah."

"We bide our time here at this Mayday Motel bullshit. We've got enough cash for a couple weeks—tops. I told you; I might know a guy that can get me a drywall job for a few days."

"Right, okay." Angie uncrossed her arms. "You always

know a guy, Joey."

"Don't trust me?"

Angie smiled. "Sure, I do."

"Let's not forget my military discount. All diners take military discounts, and the billboard on the way in said Hunky Dory's is the best diner in Florida."

"You're too much sometimes."

Josiah and Angie grew up in church families. You had the foster kids, the neighborhood kids, each with six or seven siblings. Most of them were homeschooled, and those that weren't got jobs at the church while in public high school as soon as they were old enough. Josiah and Angie worked graveyard shifts at Little Big Avenue Donuts until high school got so boring, they dropped out.

All Angie wanted to do was be a mama. Josiah wanted to be a cowboy. They were the oldest in their families. Josiah's mother took care of everybody's kids: not just the foster siblings, but all the church kids. Angie, for a long time, thought she wanted more than just a family. But then she'd met Josiah at a church picnic two summers ago, and they started getting in trouble together.

People got a sentimental look on their face when Josiah mentioned he'd served in the Marines. It made Angie proud of him. He flunked out during the end of training, but half the time the conversation didn't get that far. People didn't care, they just wanted to hear you were in the military. Be it hillbilly or cow-tipper, Bible-belter, Reformed pastor—they ate it all up. They respected the troops, especially the Marines.

"You're my personal 911 Marine," Angie cooed, tilting her head. She made her hand into a gun-shape, blowing off pretend smoke.

They began to make love as dark came over Sugar Bends. But just as things were getting started, somebody knocked on the motel door.

III

We got company," Josiah whispered, shooting up from the bed. Angie quickly threw on Josiah's red plaid shirt, and softly she reached for the .32 on the night table. Mayday Motel's flickering neon marked the tarmac outside as Josiah bent the blinds back to see who had knocked. It wasn't Mitch Johnson. He swung the door open.

Some motherfucker was standing there like a Bible salesman, smiling back at him. It was too damn late for whatever this was going to be.

"Yeah?"

"Good evening. Do you think you could do me a favor?"

The man's small marble eyes were tinted by a pair of 1950s-esque browline eyeglasses. He had smile lines for days, surrounding a neatly trimmed horseshoe mustache. Long hair swung to his shoulders, thick as a horse's black mane.

Josiah glanced back at Angie sitting on the bed. She sighed, gesturing for him to come back to bed.

"We're busy, dude. Maybe we can do this another time."

"It would just take a minute of your time, sir."

Sir. Josiah had never been called *sir* before. He looked out to the pylon in the prairie. It was dark out there. "You a cop?"

The man laughed heartily, genuinely amused. He wore a vintage rawhide jacket and blue jeans with a patched knee. "That's a first."

"Look, man, we're busy. If you're looking for cash, we're fresh broke."

"Who is it?" Angie whispered.

"Just a minute," Josiah barked.

The man scratched his head, grinning. "It's not money. I have money. Too much of it, really, for a man my age. I need some help, and, in exchange, I'll give you fifty grand and make sure Mitch Johnson of Morristown, Tennessee is out of the picture completely."

Josiah blinked. He felt his insides bunch up with worry.

"My name is Nolan."

"How do you—"

"You've got a truck parked out there that's in no shape to be road hogging anytime soon. And aren't you about two Denny's Super Slams away from having to beg for a bus pass?"

"You listenin' to us through the wall, you creep?"

Angie said, "Joey—"

Nolan smiled. His teeth were stained, lined up like yellow pearls in a tight shell. "I'm intuitive. I saw you checking in. I work around here."

"Intuitive, bullshit." Josiah hit the top of the doorframe. "How do you know about Mitch Johnson?"

"All pretty girls like your wife there got a drunk daddy like him, don't they, country boy? He calls you that—country boy. So, think you can do me that favor?"

"Look, man, I don't know what game this is, but what's the favor?"

Josiah shot a glance back at Angie, who was still sitting crisscross applesauce on the bed, gripping the handgun.

"You don't have to decide now," Nolan said. "But don't leave tomorrow. Don't leave the day after that. I'd like you to get something for me. I'll provide you with the tools and the directions."

"You a hitman?"

"Who is it, Joey?" Angie asked again.

"Some guy needs a favor."

"Remember, fifty thousand dollars. Cash. No more Mitch Johnson. You can sleep with the lights off. It's simply a favor." Nolan lifted the flip-up lens on his eyeglasses. His eyes flickered black for a moment, just a negligible, unassuming moment, but Josiah felt that flicker in his guts.

"What was—"

Nolan's marble eyes returned to normal, a dull green. He

snapped his fingers and the bedside lamp switched off. He snapped his fingers again, and it turned on.

"What the hell was that shit?" Josiah said. "Who are you? Why do you need me to do your dirty work?"

"This is the Mayday Motel, not the Four Seasons, Josiah. Sometimes a man needs a favor. And last August, you hitchhiked with your thumbs pointing up from Milwaukee to Las Vegas when that Chevy pick-up you guys haul ass in was out on commission. *That's* a man in need of a favor."

Josiah gulped; certain he saw the man's eyes go black again. He shut the door on him. Angie joined him at the window. A coyote trampled out of the tallgrass onto the tarmac. Nolan was nowhere in sight.

"Keep the gun close, Angie girl."

IV

Tricia Cross uncurled the headphones cable from the switchboard as it lit up, *On Air*. "Good evening from 101.1. I'm Tricia Cross, and right now you're either home from rush hour or clocking in at the mill. It's going to be a hot night, with a low of seventy-seven degrees, so cool off with a little Lucinda Williams until we get back."

She pulled off the headphones, smoothing down the blond hair that spilled over her shoulders, offering a flirtatious smile to Sawyer Harris, a science teacher at the middle school. She pulled him closer, hip-level to her face.

"It doesn't drive me wild knowing your husband's listening to the show while we spoon behind the scenes," Sawyer said, caressing her arms.

"You know you love it," she said in her best sultry tone.

"Are you sure about that?"

Tricia raised an eyebrow. "How much do you want to bet?"

"What have you got?"

Tricia traced her fingers along the outline of his shaft under his jeans, standing to meet him in a passionate kiss.

Sawyer let go of her embrace, gently pushing past her as the soundboard lit up, signaling two minutes until airtime. "I'm serious, Trish. You don't wonder if Fischer will suspect something and drop by unannounced? This lighthouse doesn't exactly have any hiding places."

The perks of getting involved with a middle school science teacher. Sawyer approached everything matter-of-factly, even their affair. "I don't think about it," Trish said.

She peered out the bay window at the laurel oaks scudding canopy shapes over Lake Briggs. The lighthouse was atop Devil's Hill, surrounded by mangroves and slash pines growing among driftwood. (A "lighthouse" built by the sugar mill's original owner at the turn of the century, later purchased by Tricia herself.) A barn-style bridge led to a derelict campsite that was now a parking place for teenagers and Boy Scouts. Pump Gas could be seen from the tower down Mowry Road, facing west along Barrett's Cemetery.

"So, are you going to quit seeing me, Mr. Harris?"

She admired his ass as he turned from her to gaze out the bay window at Lake Briggs. Night was falling fast. Summer was really over. He was gorgeous, she thought, and not just his sex appeal, but his gentleness too. He was a hovering six foot two with salt and pepper hair, a couple years younger than she was.

"Read my lips," Sawyer said, and they kissed again, laughing like teenagers as they kept their eyes on the switchboard for airtime.

Their affair began in May, shortly after the Hillbilly Hammer was deemed serial by authorities after the third murder. Tricia's husband was the hot-headed sheriff, Fischer Baez. She called him the "scrawny doof," though she kept that to herself. She had the displeasure of going home to Fischer at the witching hour, after her broadcast was over. Fischer wasn't a monster. He didn't punch holes in walls or throw temper tantrums like her first husband, but he was a lousy friend, and an even worse lover.

Tricia and Sawyer had known each other since high school, right around the time Tricia turned into an outsider in Sugar Bends in the late 1980s. She got pregnant in high school and stirred the rumor mill into a buzzing frenzy. Everybody believed it was Sawyer's baby (it wasn't). They said the infant would be ritualized because all those weirdos were having orgies and practicing black ceremonies.

Some of those *weirdos* would become the Scarecrows. Never mind the black masses; the group was a community watch of five: Tricia Cross, Sawyer Harris, Ben Ashcroft, Roberta Quintin, and Theo Shortridge. The Scarecrows weren't respected in Sugar Bends because of those old Satanist rumors, and in fact, most people still looked away when they saw them in public. They scared the town, those darker corners of Sugar Bends that everybody knew about but didn't acknowledge.

The Scarecrows got together every other Wednesday. Almost everybody in the group had a gift for hearing the dead, even in the smallest, most tenuous capacity. Theo Shortridge's gift was the strongest, hitting her like a shock of electricity. Tricia, on the other hand, couldn't hear the dead at all, but she shared the others' beliefs. Their relationship was a long one; they'd taken her in when she was a teenager, pregnant and alone.

Tricia had never left the Scarecrows.

She grabbed the headphones and hit the *On Air* switch. "Welcome back, that was Lucinda Williams, 'Are You Alright?'. It's half past seven and the moonlight's hiding behind the clouds from where I'm sitting. It's so quiet out there, it's almost spooky." She winked at Sawyer, and he shook his head, making a cut-it-out gesture. "Folks, this is Tricia Cross, and like I said, if you're clocking into work, I've got my phone ready, and you can text a request. I'll play whatever you like as long as it's PG-13; *only* if it's PG-13."

When she hit the switch again, Sawyer gestured to her phone on the dash.

"Your phone's blowing up." He joined her at the

soundboard.

"Fourteen requests, and only a few of them suck," Tricia said. She scrolled through the messages. She put her reading glasses on for the last one. "Huh. I don't recognize this number or name; maybe somebody from Hounds."

She showed Sawyer the screen.

Hello, Tricia Cross. My name is Nolan Craven and I really dig your show. Can you do me a favor? Can you play "Badlands" by Bruce Springsteen?

Tricia got back on air, draining coffee from her mug. "Nolan Craven, wherever you are tonight, honey, this one's for you, and you got it bad, baby, bad."

"Badlands" started, and Sawyer caressed Tricia's shoulders when she got off the air, removing her headphones for her. She programmed "Badlands" to play three times in a row.

"Come here," she said, leaving the soundboard.

He couldn't resist. Sawyer joined her on the couch.

OCTOBER 25

I

Letty and Bernie shared a chocolate milk at their lockers after homeroom. Seventh graders texted and socialized in the hall, sneaking cigarettes in the restroom. Two boys and a girl were suspended last week at Earl Jones Middle for wearing a boogeyman mask and jumping out at teachers by the cafeteria. Everybody had a joke about the Hillbilly Hammer.

"Check out old bitch Carrigan," Bernie said.

"My mom says the school board's forcing her to retire a year early," Letty said. She gulped the last of the chocolate milk. "Mom hears all kinds of inside stuff at the diner."

Carrigan was the social studies teacher. Every morning she launched into a heavy-handed lecture on the Hillbilly Hammer, grumbling about how poorly law enforcement was handling the whole thing. Her son had been a cop in Sugar Bends back in the '90s, and she never let anybody forget.

This morning, Carrigan looked extra devastated.

"She's putting the school on blast for sponsoring the Halloween fair this year. She thinks it's too soon to be having fun," Bernie said. She rubbed Vaseline up into the crevices of her arm cast. "This sucker itches something bad."

Letty snapped her locker closed. "I love fair season." She picked her messenger bag off the floor and slung it over her shoulder.

"Shoot, your mom doesn't let you walk to the mailbox, do you think she's gonna let you go play at a fair while there's a serial killer running loose?"

"Letty, Bernie," Miss Carrigan said, exiting the teacher's lounge by the lockers.

"She's a buzzkill," Bernie said, when Miss Carrigan was out of earshot.

Cameron Wheeler came around the corner with a *Rick and Morty*-stickered skateboard under his arm, grabbing the empty chocolate milk carton out of Letty's hand. He flattened it on his forehead, then gave it back to her.

"Hey, Cam," Letty said.

"Sup."

Bernie slapped Cameron on the back. "Seen any killers lately?"

"I'm laughing my ass off. Grow a pair, Bernadette," Cameron retorted. He had a sandy- blond comb-over and recently started wearing musky cologne to school.

Their best bud was popular lately, but not in a good way.

Cameron had gotten a reputation for being a wuss after word got out that he dialed 911 on Labor Day weekend. He'd sworn up and down he saw the Hillbilly Hammer on his front porch, trying to break into his house. After a brief investigation, cops found nothing, not even footprints on the steps.

"Let me ask you something, Cam. Think your mom's gonna let you hit up the Halloween fair this year with us? Well, with me—I don't think Letty's going."

"I *am* going," Letty said. "Shit, you guys."

Cameron picked his skateboard up off the linoleum and slapped it against Brittney Parker's locker, who gave him an unforgiving glare. "What fair? There's still the stupid curfew. There's not going to be any fair."

"Nope, Ferris wheel's up," Bernie said.

Brittney nudged herself into their triangle. "Talking to the dead again, Letty Hardin?"

"Maybe," Letty said. "Right now, in fact. You're dead to me."

"When your dad died, guess he took your manners with him. Bitch."

When Brittney Parker walked away toward the algebra room, trailing glitter, Bernie hooted. "Wow, she's really talking out of her ass lately."

Letty shrugged. "A medium's work is never easy."

"You're a medium now?" Cameron said. He and Bernie exchanged glances.

"Communicating with the dead is what mediums do, so—" Letty smiled. "Yes, I'm practicing being a medium."

"I like you, Letty. You're a go-getter weirdo," Bernie said.

"You didn't seem to think it was so weird two nights ago in the cemetery. Didn't you get any vibes from Babes Henry when you got home?"

Bernie scrunched her face. "Like, dead girl vibes?"

"Her presence," Letty said.

"Sure, Letty, I'm sure I did," she said appealingly.

Letty's reputation could be summed up by the taunting seventh graders jabbing whispers behind her back with the snide phrase, *Letty sees dead people.* "I don't *see* them, I hear them," she used to correct her classmates. She liked feeling different from the other kids. Sometimes different was better, even at the expense of fitting in.

Letty knew she wasn't the only weirdo freak residing in Sugar Bends. There was the community watch thing too, the Scarecrows. Everybody talked about them even if nobody knew what the heck they were up to, except maybe some weird sex stuff in the woods. But lately, Letty, Bernie, and Cameron had changed their minds about the Scarecrows being weirdos: when the school board denied Babes Henry a dedicated garden in the schoolyard, the Scarecrows went and planted her a garden.

Parents were up in arms about the garden getting installed by the Scarecrows. Some folks were so pissed off that they volunteered to plant the dedication themselves—anything to keep the corrupt sex-crazed group away from the school. But the school board shunned the parents due to fear the attention would influence the killer. Scarecrows showed up and did it anyway, and were now up to their necks in zoning fees, whatever that meant. Letty didn't know or care, but she and her friends thought what they did was awesome.

The Scarecrows were another mystery for the town, interesting enough for Letty, Bernie, and Cameron to discuss until the cows came home.

The friends walked down the trophy hall toward the science room. There was a display case stuffed with love letters and teddy bears dedicated to Babes Henry.

"We still on tomorrow for the online *Magic: The Gathering* tournament?" Bernie said.

"Actually," Letty said. "I made plans to hit up the cemetery after my mom crashes. Kinda important I be there . . . at the cemetery."

Cameron raspberried his exasperation. "Seriously?"

"Don't bust my chops," Letty said.

"It costs twenty-five dollars each just to *join* the tournament," Bernie said. "If you think you're getting your money back—"

"I don't, Bern, okay? I just got other things to do than play video games."

"Yeah," Bernie mumbled. "Talk to the dead."

In class, their earth science teacher, Mr. Sawyer Harris, handed out a pop quiz on climate change. He'd been easy on the class for the last two weeks after Babes Henry's murder, but assignments were starting to return to normal. He was Letty's favorite teacher by a longshot. He wasn't pervy or condescending. His desk was covered in hard drives, papers, and Magic Markers.

"Let's just see where we're at," Mr. Sawyer said, passing out the worksheets. "When you're done with the quiz, flip it over, and we'll have a brief discussion."

"Psst," Letty whispered to her friends sitting in the row in front of her. "He's a Scarecrow. I know he is."

Bernie glanced over her shoulder. "How do you know?"

"No talking during the quiz, please," Mr. Sawyer said.

After the lunch bell rang, Letty approached Mr. Sawyer's desk. "Mr. Sawyer—"

"Miss Hardin."

"Mr. Sawyer, do you know who the Scarecrows are?"

"I beg your pardon?"

"The Scarecrows; the neighborhood watch everybody talks about."

Mr. Sawyer's gaze turned earnest and said, "I fail to see what that has to do with kinetic energy and climate change." He took a ballpoint pen from behind his ear. "Okay, Miss Hardin, the Scarecrows are a campfire story, a tall tale. What's the matter?"

"But, Mr. Sawyer, I know it's more than that. I've heard the rumors. It's not all bad, but it's not good either, if you know what I mean. My mom once said it was satanic."

He stifled a chuckle. "Miss Hardin, I think this is out of place."

"Please, I know you know because I know . . . well—" Letty's voice trailed off, gazing down at her sneakers. "I know the Scarecrows are real and some kids say you're one of them. You go to meetings and stuff when the moon gets full. Everybody talks about it. My neighbor— she's one of them. She let it slip once."

"I see."

"The reason I'm asking is because if you guys are really a neighborhood watch, then you'll find the killer, and everything can go back to normal again for all of us. And we'll get the Halloween fair on top of it."

"I see." Mr. Sawyer smiled.

"A lot of us are counting on you, even if you are a teacher during the day."

Mr. Sawyer double-clicked the ballpoint pen, replacing it behind his ear. "I think no more discussions out of that deck. This is a classroom, Miss Hardin." He showed Letty to the door. "How did you do on today's quiz?"

"Fine," she said.

Letty always spied on her neighbors and teachers, even before her dad died, and she spent summers climbing the southern oaks to see over people's paddock fences and mango trees. Theo Shortridge was her favorite person to spy on. She'd seen Mr. Sawyer and Theo together often—not romantically, because Theo was married to the plant nursery woman, Nancy—but in their Scarecrow-working manner. Mr. Sawyer lived in the Tidioute trailer park, deep in the woods on the east side of town.

Letty believed she'd join the Scarecrows one day. Or maybe she'd make her own Talking Dead Neighborhood Watch.

Maybe there was more to life than secret clubs. Maybe Bernie was right. Maybe talking to the dead was getting old and she'd been playing make believe all this time. After all, she hadn't heard from her father in months.

Letty had her own secret club for the time being. She joined her friends on the athletic field under the bleachers when everybody was already eating lunch. Under a scrim of clouds, the heat was still sweltering, and the controlled burnings at the mill gave Sugar Bends a smokey, stale fragrance.

Cameron waved Letty over. "Since I left my *Magic: The Gathering* cards at home, you got the Ouija board today?"

Letty sat between her friends in the high grass, pulling off her messenger bag. She unwrapped a tomato and mayo sandwich. "I'm giving up on Ouija boards. It's just an old parlor game."

"Letty Hardin, growing up right before our eyes," Bernie laughed, opening a can of pop.

"You shits are being real jerks," said Letty.

"Come on, Let, we're just playing with you."

"Yeah," Cameron said. "Hey, I've got something." He pulled a Spiderman wallet out of his shorts pocket, handing over a mid-2000s photograph printed on stock paper. "That's her. That's my grandma."

Letty smiled. "You really loved her."

"She died when I was eight. Cancer. Did you need to know that for the séance?"

Letty passed the photograph to Bernie. "You still want to do the séance? You guys have ragged on me all day."

"Chillax," Cameron said. "I told you we were playing."

"Talking Dead Society rules," Bernie said.

"Okay." Letty dusted sandwich crumbs off her pants. "But we all have to hold hands."

They took turns looking at the picture of Cameron and his elderly, smiling grandmother face- up in the weeds. Letty closed her eyes and filled her lungs with warm air. Cameron and Bernie followed suit.

"Your grandmother's name was—what was it, Cam?" Letty asked.

She knew the soft humming wasn't going to itch her inner ear today. It hadn't in so long, and no matter how many séances she held with her friends, or cemetery-jaunting she did, she couldn't make it happen.

"Angela."

"Angela. Angela says . . . she says she loves you."

"You can see her? Does she look sick? Last time I saw her she was pale."

"No, she's—"

"We got a visitor," Bernie said, breaking their triangle.

Brick Myers, the biggest bully at Earl Jones Middle, rolled up on a cobalt-chromed kick scooter, off the asphalt and into the grass. He hurled a stink bomb toward the bleachers. It smelled like motor oil but didn't ignite all the way.

"You're an ass," Bernie said. "Real mature."

"We live in the dickhole of this country. That was nothing," Brick said.

Brick's brother, Everett, was in a high school gang with three other guys, the Timbers. They'd vandalized the vacant mall off River Cross, graffitied the rest stop near the sugarcane fields, and gotten drunk and arrested at Sugar Bends Park. They pissed everybody off. Brick was a fuckhead in training.

"Playing *Dora, the Dead Explorer* again?" Brick said. "What happened to your twelve by ten hideaway you hawked from the dump?"

"Storm," Cameron said. "We didn't bother rebuilding it. What the hell do you care?"

But that wasn't true. Letty's mom made them take it down after the curfew was installed. They spent part of July building it down by the old campsite on Devil's Hill.

"Buzz the hell off, Brick," Cameron said.

"Come suck my dick."

"You're not my type, dillweed."

Brick was fast on that kick scooter, and sometimes it was just best to get the fight over with. He was one of those kids that drew on himself all the time, stars and dicks, footballs, crossbones. He sported a textured quiff hairstyle like his brother.

"You know you three are real cumdumps, you know that?"

"Asshole," Cameron said.

"Yeah, your mom ate mine for breakfast."

"Make fun of us all you want, Brick Myers, but if you know anybody that's died that you'd like to communicate with one last time, I'll do it for free," Letty said. "It's called networking."

"Do you suck dick after?"

Letty rolled her eyes, grabbing her messenger bag so it wasn't crushed beneath his kick scooter. "No, I don't." Brick tried rolling over her hand, but the kids stood, fists at their side like they'd ever thrown a fist in their life. They hadn't fought much except to defend each other.

"You gonna hit me?" Brick hissed. "You think I'm the Hillbilly Hammer playing hopscotch on your porch, Cammy?"

"Get lost," Cameron said.

"No, you get lost. Stay off my turf or I'll throw a stink bomb through your mom's bedroom window."

Brick spit in their direction, knocked over Bernie's can of pop, and rode away when he saw his friends. The only sound was the softball coach's shouts in the distance.

Letty took Cameron's hand. "You, okay?"

"I'm fine. He's a jerk-ass."

Bernie sighed, looking over her shoulder. She used her good arm to pat the grass and dirt off their backsides. "We believe you, Cam. About the Hillbilly Hammer. Right, Letty?"

"Yes."

Cameron laughed, picking up his bookbag. "I believe me too."

"Talking Dead Society rules again," Bernie quipped.

Letty put her arms around her friends, and they walked toward the homeroom.

When the last school bell rang, the three friends managed to avoid Brick Myers. Letty's mouth was parched from the smokey heat as they talked shit about Old Bitch Carrigan while she drove, hunched over the wheel, out of the faculty parking lot.

The sugarcane burnings lasted from October through May, with the stale odor creeping into the new harvest. Everybody in Sugar Bends called it the *black rain*. When black rain season was upon the town, it meant tractors making noise in the middle of the night, pulling up in hopper trailers to ship the stalks of sugarcane from the conveyor belts in the mill to the refinery out in Tallahassee. Sometimes the sky did bleed black rain, of course, but it was just a variation of smog, perspiring into flecks of gray as it descended from a long day in the high heat. Baked grass made the smoke fragrance worse.

Letty's dad had been a harvester. He worked in the mill, operating forklifts and combine harvesters. The mill had its share of darkness, just like the town. In 1988, a man burned to death during a controlled burning after an altercation with a fellow from the mill. The story hadn't changed much over the years; fists flew, pride was bigger than reason, and the guy accidentally set fire to himself instead of the stalks growing out of the soiled ground.

The mill's burning man barely scratched the surface of Sugar Bends's dark history. The sun set earlier in Sugar Bends, by twenty-four minutes. Some of the Boonies liked to say it was because of the layout of the sugarcane fields: twelve-and-a-half miles long, harvested too close to swamp ash, like a blip in the matrix of meteorology. Some townspeople, if not most, said it was a mistake to study the reasons too closely.

Lightning strikes were commonplace, too. The railroad

tracks up near the logging yard and the exit to Hounds regularly saw a plume of purple flame engulfing the tracks like sparkling dust. Nobody had gotten close enough to it to know if it was dangerous or just a trick of the light preceding a torrential rainstorm. There'd been sightings of a rabid sea creature in Lake Briggs. A man had killed the thing with a shotgun after it attacked his granddaughter. You could catch eels and viper fish in that lake. Weird markings had been found all over the logging yard. Disappearances weren't common, but they weren't unheard of, either.

One locally famous kidnapping happened to a seventh grader in their class, Lydia Mann. She'd been kidnapped as a small child and not rescued until a year later. She'd been mostly unharmed, but it was another dark story for the town, and one Letty's mom never let her forget. (She'd made Letty invite Lydia to all her birthday parties since.)

There was roadkill everywhere in Sugar Bends, no matter how little traffic the town got any given season: porcupines, gators, opossums and rabbits, iguanas, even coyotes.

Off the skirts of I-75 was what folks called Sidewinder, a winding nine-mile road connecting Hounds and Sugar Bends. The town's economy used to depend on a factory that employed three-quarters of Hounds and Sugar Bends combined during the plastics boom in the 1970s Hounds. It closed for good in 2020, and the town's separated economies inserted tension in both directions.

The heart of Sugar Bends was on Placerville Rd. You had Sugar's Market, the only grocer, for twelve miles unless you drove up north of Hounds to another market. It was where the town *lived*, by the movie theater, sheriff's department, diner and bars, laundromat, St. Ruth's Catholic Church, pawnshop, and the drugstore. The schools and post office were near the park and athletics building, alongside River Cross: a true canal with gloomy green water.

The Bends Mall, like the campsite off Griffin and Devil's Hill, closed in 2011. Layers of dirt clung to the splintered cracks through the concrete foundation, and the pine trees and agave had to be hauled away from damage every hurricane season. From Barrett's Woods to Mayday Motel, everything was obscenely rustic and baked in the sun.

Midafternoon, Letty, Bernie, and Cameron strolled into Sugar's Market, next door to the diner. It was crawling with people. "There she goes, old bitch Carrigan, buying her head of lettuce and talcum powder," Cameron said.

"She probably needs prunes," Bernie said. "She can't shit without them."

"She's plugged up," Letty laughed.

Spying on Miss Carrigan after school meant watching her from afar as they bought candy, poking fun at her perpetual grimace as she navigated the market with a shopping cart. The kids bought pop and Skittles to eat on the way home.

They walked the long way because it was only Wednesday. They had the whole rest of the week to hurry up and do homework, and watch their parents worry about a serial killer. They were supposed to continue a game of *Magic: The Gathering* at Bernie's, but Letty's mom was off work today and she'd want her home early. There was always tomorrow. It was the most satisfying thing in Letty's life, she thought. The promise of tomorrow with her friends. It felt like summer for a hot minute.

As the afternoon wore on, the kids found themselves at Pump Gas on Mowry Road, where the lighthouse could be seen from the flatwood prairie and street. They sat on the curb, drinking pop. One of the old-timers in Sugar Bends, a guy named Ben Ashcroft the kids had spied on from time to time, owned Pump Gas. He was friendly enough, but Letty was skeptical. He was *a* Scarecrow, and *positively* into some satanic ritual stuff. His niceness was just a mask. You had to watch out and carry that pepper spray.

Ben Ashcroft wasn't around that hot afternoon, though. The road was mostly free of low-rumble traffic. Letty noticed a man standing out in the tallgrass by an electric pylon. His black hair whipped over his face even though there wasn't a breeze. She blinked, feeling nervously frozen from the bizarre stranger, and he became giant. He was taller than the pylon itself, larger than life.

"Hey, guys—" Letty started.

The man wore a rawhide jacket and had a black mustache. He had old-time eyeglasses with big, round frames. Suddenly, he shrunk back to normal size, and Letty blinked, trying to register the transformation. The man snapped his fingers and the clear lenses flipped open, black eyes glowing back at her. He snapped his fingers again and the lenses closed.

"What the—"

Around the corner of Pump Gas, a red sports car flew onto the road and flashed their high beams in the kids' faces. It was the Timber gang.

"Hey, nerd-holes," said Everett Myers. The other guys were in the back: Lisle Baruso, J.T. Alvarez, and Brent Lowe.

"Did you see that?" Letty said. "That guy out there—"

"What guy?" Bernie said. "In the field?"

"Yeah, he was huge, like, tall, and he was staring at me."

Lisle scoffed. "Nerd-holes, you better watch your backs 'cuz the Hillbilly Hammer's been chomping at the bit to pull that hammer out. Babes Henry, now she was a catch. J.T. here got his fingers wet the night before she got slaughtered."

"Nobody asked," Bernie said. "Let her rest in peace, huh?"

"Ignore 'em," Cameron said. "They're just trying to rile us up."

Everett blew a kiss at the three of them. "Give me that pop. I don't feel like stretching my legs just to get a drink. Give me yours—that one, there."

"You're kidding, bro," Bernie said. "You owe me two bucks."

"Just give it to him. It's too hot to run," Cameron said.

Bernie clicked her tongue, handing over the cold can to Everett in the front seat.

"Thanks for playing," Everett laughed, popping open the can and drinking half of it.

Bernie and Cameron threw insults at the Timbers as Everett hit the gas on that old sports car so hard, it went into second gear and a cloud of dust billowed down the road and into their perspiring faces.

"Letty? Hey, earth to Letty. What's she looking at?" Cameron said, dusting road dirt off his t-shirt.

Letty was paralyzed in fear as the black-haired stranger continued to burn his cold, hard, slack-faced stare into her. His collar moved in an invisible breeze, a wind she didn't feel that hot autumn day. He had the worst grimace Letty had ever seen in her life. She flinched, trying not to look.

"You don't see that guy in the grass over thataways?" Letty asked.

"I don't see anything," Bernie said. "Where?"

By the time Letty returned her focus to the tallgrass prairie, he was gone.

II

Theo had stood in the kitchen making dinner when she noticed the silhouette of the neighbor girl on the dark shaded screen in her Florida room. "Letty?" She opened the door, surprised to see her. Letty stood on the broken, sea green-accented steps, binoculars hanging around her neck.

"My mom, she got called in to work the night shift. And I got the creeps all of a sudden, so I came outside for a minute, but I locked myself out."

Theo hitched her chin. "Okay. I can pry open a window or something. Come in for a minute and I'll walk with you back over."

Letty walked with Theo, looking over the punk and new wave records framed on the wall. Letty's skin was buttery. She was so young, not more than twelve or thirteen years old. She'd told her once, but Theo forgot. "You, okay?" Theo asked.

"My mom will have a cow if I break a window."

The house smelled like cumin and chili powder. It was rare Theo cooked for herself nowadays, but she was getting tired of BBQ takeout. She walked into the kitchen to turn off the stove burner.

"Is that 101.1 you're listening to?" Letty asked. "Tricia

Cross talks more than she plays songs."

"Sometimes it's nice listening to somebody else do the talking," Theo said.

Letty tucked hair strands behind her ear. "My mom doesn't think there should be a radio show going on at a time like this."

"I'll give you some chili to take back to your mom." Theo scooped a generous serving into a dish, clasping the lid shut. "Come on, let's go."

Their two cracker houses looked identical from the outside, except for the differential blue and green-accented wood framing. The yards were full of weeds amid dwarf shrubs and sun-bleached sabal palms. The crabgrass hadn't been trimmed since August. Most of the houses on Loxahatchee Road were like that. In the back by a mango tree, Nancy had built a tool shed for both families to use. Letty's house had a washing machine in the back under an aluminum awning that rang like a tin drum when it rained.

"All of your windows are locked?" Theo asked.

"I think so."

Theo climbed the concrete steps up to Letty's kitchen door, noticing the windows still taped with aluminum foil from the inside. Theo used to think Jane did that to keep the poorly-insulated house cool, but now it was clear she just didn't want anybody peeping in. She tried lifting a window frame. It didn't budge.

"So, is it true? You talk to the dead?" Letty said.

Theo looked over her shoulder at this subversively charming kid. Simultaneously, she was tired from work, wanted to down a quarter of a half-gallon bottle of bourbon, and was not in the mood.

"Let's go around front," Theo said.

The sun had set an hour ago, and the only functional streetlights on Loxahatchee Road were four houses down. The floodlights coming from Theo's Florida room were bright enough to give anyone a migraine. She kept them on for Nancy in case she returned. *When* she returned.

"You let it slip once, you know," Letty said, following at her heels. "Well, Nancy did. Ever since then I've watched you, because I have the same power."

"Did Nancy also tell you she had an overactive imagination?" Theo smiled.

The front windows were bathed in brass lamp light. A round pumpkin was lit up by candlelight in the sill, a sharp grin carved into its skin. The light in the quiet nighttime comforted Theo as she climbed the broken steps to the dark shaded porch. "Give me a hand; let's lift this."

Letty joined her, and with a one-two count they lifted the wood frame, but it didn't budge. "We're not tall enough for the windows on the side of the house. I don't have a ladder."

Theo sighed, wiping her forehead with the back of her hand. It was a sticky night, not a breeze in the air.

"You can tell me," Letty said. "I won't tell. I'm like you."

Theo tried lifting the other window. "I don't talk to the dead, but I can hear them."

"Can you hear my dad?"

Theo glanced at her, lowering her voice. "When did your father die?"

"Two years and four months ago."

Theo's mood darkened, and she wished she hadn't admitted to anything. Sometimes shit just came out of her mouth. She wiped her perspiring forehead again. She recalled Jane's grief, that screeching sound of agony that had come from the house. It was horrible. She and Nancy held each other, glad it wasn't them the great loss had happened to. They made a maudlin fool's promise they'd die together, on the same day, the same hour, their heartbeats quitting in synchronous love. It was the kind of remark couples made with each other, but the memory made her sick to her stomach.

Theo tried the front door, and it gave and opened. It wasn't locked.

"Thanks, Theo. I probably should've tried that," Letty said.

Theo laughed. "Hey, it's okay. Nice jack-o-lantern you got there. You give that chili to your mom, okay?"

"I will ... so, do you? Talk to the dead?" Letty asked, as Theo turned back toward her house.

"I can hear them. Sometimes." Theo waved to a man across the sidewalk walking his black lab. It was comforting seeing somebody else. Curfew started soon.

"What's it sound like?"

"Like . . . bumblebees in my ear."

"My therapist, Mrs. Sanders, she thinks it's healthy I think I have this power. My mom makes me do sessions with her."

"How's that working out?"

"Not so good. Mrs. Sanders says what I want to hear. She's okay, I guess. She has trust issues."

"That's everybody. Look, Letty, I think you should go back inside and lock the door. It's getting late."

Letty agreed, walking through the doorway. She shut the screen door but turned back around as Theo started down the steps. "Theo? Can you hear my dad?"

"I'm not sure."

"Let me know if you do, okay?"

Theo smiled gently. "Scout's honor. You lock that door."

"Theo?"

"Yes?"

"I saw something today. It gave me the creeps, but if my mom finds out, I won't be able to go anywhere ever again because she'll flip her lid. My friend, Bernie Acosta, thinks I'm crazy."

"Well, what did you see?" Theo crossed her arms, moving up a step. The floodlights flickered on.

"There was a man in the fields looking at me near the gas station. He had this mean look. Like, he was mad at me. His eyes—well, he looked like a creeper."

Theo arched her eyebrows. A hot breeze flushed her cheeks. "Did he say anything to you?"

"No. He was too far away."

"You listen to that mama of yours until this town's back to normal, okay? If he was by the gas station, he's probably one of the drunks that hangs out there in the fields and up by the camp. I'll keep a lookout."

"Hey, you *are* a Scarecrow."

Theo waved, heading down the steps when Letty stuck her face out the front door.

"Theo? Do you think they'll catch the killer?"

"I hope so."

Theo watched Letty close the door. She heard the lock bracket in place, and as soon as she turned toward her own house, the static electricity hummed in her ears. The hairs on her arms stood up. Letty's dad was all around her. He was everywhere. He'd been in the walls, in the grass, swimming all over the perimeter, warm and loving, and everywhere. He was everywhere.

Theo smiled, bolting her front door.

OCTOBER 26

I

Josiah slumped in a corner booth watching Angie drink cherry cola with extra ice as Glen Campbell's voice drifted through Hunky Dory's diner singing, "Gentle on My Mind." The Chevy was kaput. The battery was dead; the engine wouldn't do more than tick. They'd walked to the diner from Mayday Motel, crossing over the railroad tracks and River Cross to Placerville. Paper skeletons hung on the windows and foam spiders were draped over the cash register. Halloween was coming.

They'd stopped into Sugar's Market on the way to the diner to ask if there was an auto body shop around. There was: Arnie's, all the way by Mell's Citrus and Nursery, and it would be a five-mile walk to get to it. Unless a mechanic gave them the deal of a lifetime, they didn't have enough money for a car battery.

"Baby," Angie said, scooting into him. She kissed the corner of his mouth. "I got some bad news. I got my period this morning."

He'd wanted the baby to look like him.

Josiah put his arm around Angie. "I'm not mad."

"You're not?"

"Hell no."

Weeks ago, on the last day of summer up in Arkansas Hills, Josiah and Angie sat in a diner eating off the five-dollar all-day breakfast menu. He promised her he was going to get soft when he became a dad. No more lonesome cowboy. Talk to Jesus more. Find a real job and fix up that Chevy.

"Think you'll love the baby more than me?"

"I could never love anybody more than you, Angie Johnson."

They kissed as the waitress came to take their order. Her name tag read "Jane." She'd probably waited tables her whole life, Josiah thought. The Glen Campbell song playing was made for times like these: thinking about where to run to and how to stop life from going too quickly.

"Jane, if you don't mind me saying so, you look like a Chuck Berry song," Josiah winked.

Jane smiled. "I'll take that as a compliment."

"You better." Josiah lifted his cherry cola and shook the ice. "We'll take cheeseburgers and fries."

When she left with their order, Josiah's eyes flared, still furious about the truck. Angie squeezed his thigh under the booth.

"How will we get Halloween costumes if we don't got a car?" Angie asked.

"Halloween's for sinners."

"I know, but free candy isn't."

"When that Chevy's purring with a new battery in her, you can have all the candy you want."

Angie sighed, gazing down at her fingernails. "I was gonna tell you, Joey, I was thinking last night I'd call my cousin Billy in Little Rock. Maybe he can wire us the money."

Josiah uncurled his arm from her, frowning sharply. "You call Billy, then Billy calls my mama, then Mama calls the church, then the church calls the cops. Then Ramblin' Man finds us and drops us in a ditch. You got those two thousand dollars, Angie?"

"No."

"You got an excuse for us takin' peanut butter and bread and beer from that Walmart?"

"No."

"Don't talk to nobody."

Silence fell over the booth. He owed this drywall job to Angie, and to their marriage. But for a guy that owed him a favor, a whole damn job, Todd Milano hadn't returned his phone calls and for all Josiah knew, the guy moved back to Morristown or Milwaukee, fell off the face of the earth.

Josiah said, "I'll call the guy when we get back to the motel."

"Promise, Joey?"

"Cross my heart, on George Jones's grave."

"And it'll be just like we dreamed about. You'll go to work doing your drywall. I'll have dinner waiting for you when you come home in your dirty coveralls. A beer and me. How does that sound?"

"Sounds real nice."

"You're romantic. You got that."

Their conversation was broken by the jingle of the bell at the diner door.

"Hey, Joey, there's that guy," Angie said. "Nolan."

"Son of a bitch is back."

Nolan. Nolan with his favors and spooky black eyes, hands balled into fists down at his sides. He had the build and shape of a primitive hunter or professional boxer. His rawhide jacket clung to his muscular and tight form. He looked like he would take a swing or two if you looked at him the wrong way in the checkout line.

"He don't even know we're here," Josiah said. "He's probably a voyeur sex-freak. That's why he was listenin' in on us through the walls at that fleabag motel."

"What's a voyeur sex-freak?"

Josiah pulled his Chevron ball cap down, his sandy-blond hair sticking out the sides, as Jane brought their food.

"Here's your cheeseburgers, kids. You better eat your greens when you get home," she said.

"Miss Chuck Berry," Josiah said. "Have you seen that gentleman over yonder by the cash drawer before? See—with the long hair? He comin' in here all the time?"

Jane glanced over her shoulder at the front of the diner. "I can't say that I have. But, you know what, I've never seen the likes of you two before either. He just paid your tab, by the way. Nice guy."

Josiah and Angie exchanged tight expressions, as Jane winked, leaving them to their lunch.

"Hey, look, here he comes," Angie said.

Nolan waltzed up to the jukebox, picking Bruce Springsteen's "Badlands." When the snare kicked in, he flashed a contemptuous smile, and came toward their booth. For a split second, Josiah saw Nolan appear ceiling-high, towering over their dimly lit booth so he and Angie were covered in his shadow. Josiah gasped, grabbing his forehead as if struck by a blow. Nolan returned to normal height.

"Feeling okay, country boy? You look pale," Nolan said. "You don't have a case of the –'rona virus, do you?"

"What do you want?" Josiah said. *What the hell just happened?* he thought.

Nolan slid into the booth across from them. "This is one of my favorite old tunes. The Boss starts telling us there's trouble in the heartland, but boy howdy, you're not ready for him preaching. He's *spitting* at them badlands. He's so mad. But he doesn't sing it mad. Must have been a hard sell."

"I'm going to ask you again," Josiah stammered. Angie shook in his arms. "What do you want?"

"The badlands," Nolan narrowed his eyes coyly, tucking a strand of thick, black hair behind his ear. "You kids got it bad. You're outlaws."

"You gonna rob us, mister? We don't have two dimes to rub together," Angie said.

Nolan sipped Angie's cherry soda. He drank almost the entire glass. "Tastes different than it used to. A long time ago they used real sugar. Nowadays, everything tastes like aspartame."

"So why us, huh?" Josiah said. "You still haven't answered me. You're just going to hand over fifty grand to us—for what?"

Nolan cleared his throat, folding his hands in front of him. "It's like I told you, you're outlaws. You need money and I have money to give, but I'm also in need of a favor. I'd like for you to retrieve something for me at Barrett's Cemetery, about six miles west of here. Almost the same distance you walked today."

Nolan snapped his fingers. Black balloons dropped from the ceiling in slow-moving succession. Josiah and Angie gasped, holding onto one another as the balloons gently fell. The other patrons seemed not to notice.

Nolan's voice changed. His tone deepened into a sinister, deep register. He frowned. "I want you to get me the headstone of a young woman that recently died. Her name is Margot 'Babes' Henry. Her grave is fresh, the limestone hasn't set in the dirt yet. You won't need all the muscle in the world to lift it out, but you'll need a good shovel and the right gloves. You'll retrieve the shovel and gloves at a rest stop on the edge of town everybody around here calls The Pits. Kids play there, but it's mostly forgotten. You'll return to Barrett's Cemetery and remove the headstone, hump it back to the motel, and I'll come by the next morning to get it."

Josiah grunted fearfully. Angie gulped as a black balloon floated into her lap.

"The balloons," Josiah uttered.

"A headstone from the cemetery," Angie said. "But why?"

Nolan's voice returned to its normal register. "Your pretty little head only must entertain the notion that your daddy, Mitch Johnson, won't ever be a problem for you ever again. He's looking for you right now." He grinned scornfully. "He's out on the hog—the Ramblin' Man, headed south. He knows you're in Florida. It's only a matter of time before he finds out where."

"Alright, mister, so we get this headstone. We go to this Pits place and suddenly we're not outlaws no more? We're gonna grave rob and you're gonna take away all our problems? Seems generous," Josiah said. "How do you know all this shit about us?"

Nolan drank the rest of Angie's cherry cola. He smoothed down his horseshoe mustache. Josiah thought he looked like a 1967 Western album cover.

"I'm older than I look. My heart is old. I burned nearly to death at the sugarcane mill in 1988—nearly. I wasn't much older than the two of you. I survived, left town, and it took me a decade to realize I wasn't aging. I was the same man in 1988 as I was in 1998, and 2008, and today."

"You're . . . dead," Angie whispered.

"No, I'm not dead. I'm sitting in this booth at this diner with you, very much alive. Since that winter morning I went up in flames, I've had this gift to *psychic*. I can hear it all. It's riveting, really. Gray matter doesn't just sift away. Gray matter is like your soul, and the more I can hear, the stronger I get. I'm growing all the time. Small towns like Sugar Bends, they're vulnerable places."

Angie closed her eyes. "Make it go away. Knock his block off, Joey. *Please*. Please stop."

Nolan continued. "There's a woman that lives in this town. Her name is Theo Shortridge. Her psychic ability is stronger than mine. I want it. I need to find her and absorb her shadow, her loud grief, her voice, her bones. But there's a few of you— outlaws—that I've picked up on. I've picked up on the Chevy, and the Ramblin' Man, and that farmhouse you're dreaming of, Angie Johnson. The one with the porch swing. I'm Badlands, times five."

"You know the one," Angie said.

"I do."

"Please, mister, you're scaring—"

"The pants off of you?" Nolan smiled.

The black balloons stopped floating.

"You can hear the dead and it gives you magic powers to

throw party balloons, is that it?" Josiah barked. "You're a carnival freak. What if we say no? What if I put a boot up your ass right now?"

Nolan lifted his lenses. His eyes flickered black. They gasped.

"Then Mitch Johnson will break down that motel room door and put a bullet in your shoulder. Then you got real problems. Angie, you'll be working for tips at that little donut shop, going home to your daddy every night, never going nowhere else but to church. You'd face some jail time, too. That'll make a pleasant Christmas card."

Nolan's eyes returned their slack-faced stares as he lowered the lenses. "You're outlaws," he continued. "I've bludgeoned six people in the skull with a titanium hammer, just hard enough that their eye sockets snap, and paralysis consumes them. You should see it. One eyeball dangling from the optic nerve, throbbing into eventual blindness. Of course, they die before blindness kicks in. I've done it for two decades, and I'll do it for hundreds more. I'm afraid, son, you don't have much choice in the matter. You and your wife."

Josiah shook his head. "Don't you scare her like that."

"Joey, we're gonna do what he says," Angie cried.

Josiah side-eyed the other diner patrons. Nobody seemed

to notice their outburst, the tears, or the balloons strewn all over the table and floor. It was like they were by themselves.

"What if a pig's out patrolling, huh? What do I do then? I can't even get a traffic ticket, man, I've got a misdemeanor back home in Tennessee."

"Two, actually." Angie corrected.

"Uh-oh," Nolan said. "Dangerous country, cowboy. You let me worry about police patrol. You'll do just fine. Mitch Johnson will be history, and you'll walk away with fifty thousand dollars. Just sitting with you here right now in this mom-and-pop diner, I'm absorbing your frequencies, the fear and miles you've gone." He exhaled, looking out the window. "Can you do me this favor?"

Josiah and Angie, wide-eyed and trembling, nodded. "Do it, Joey. We need the money. Not like we got a choice."

"Fine. But there's one thing you didn't answer."

Nolan's eyes flickered. "What's that?"

"Why us?" Josiah asked.

"I told you. You're outlaws," Nolan said. "You want a farmhouse where you can bounce a baby on your knee? You'll do whatever I ask you to because you don't got no other choice. We both win."

"You're the goddamn devil," Josiah whimpered.

Nolan shook the ice, now spiked red from the cherry cola, and set down the glass. "Thanks for the pop. Would a devil do this?"

A stack of neat hundred-dollar bills appeared in both of his palms. Josiah and Angie wailed at the sight.

"I'm a man of my word," Nolan said. "But I'm not the devil. Go ahead, outlaws. Take from my left hand—go now, take it."

It took them a minute to gather their nerves, but Angie ribbed Josiah and they reached for the cash out of Nolan's grasp. The two poorest outlaws in Sugar Bends had money in their hands.

"The other half," Nolan started. "The cash in my right palm will be yours once you've executed the favor. When I get the headstone, the money will be yours."

The money disappeared into thin air. There was no blackout, no flash, it just went away as if it had never been there at all.

"Well," Nolan said. "My Bruce song is over. Guess that means I'll leave you. But I'll be around. You know what to do."

Nolan's eyes glowed black, just briefly under those browline eyeglasses of his. He screamed, falling backward in fright. This time, everybody in the diner turned around to look.

"Did you see it?" Josiah said. "His eyes. They turned black!"

Angie stuffed the money into her handbag so nobody would see. "We do this one favor, and we get the hell outta this town."

The jingle bell sounded again. Foam spiders and paper skeletons shook as Nolan walked out of Hunky Dory's and onto the sidewalk. Josiah and Angie clung to each other.

Meanwhile, Jane, clearing the dishes off the bar counter, called out to a busboy. "Hey, Wallace, gimme a broom, will you? There's black confetti all over the floor. Jerk kids."

Black Rain Season - Kayli Scholz

82

II

Jane Hardin idled in front of St. Ruth's Catholic Church in her trusty '06 Volvo. The church needed a facelift. The blue hyacinths that usually bloomed in late summer and fall hadn't been tended to. The planters in the pathway were empty of soil and an unwelcoming church sign stood sun-damaged in a staggerbush.

It was the stained glass windows Jane missed. She missed seeing Saint Margaret and Jesus catch the light, the mahogany wood frame inside the church cradling it all. It was comforting to see, even from the safety of the Volvo. She missed the sense of community attending church gave her. She missed the Lord's Prayer. But today had been ten hours on her feet with less in tips than the night before, and she was aching to get home and tear off her polyester pink and white uniform. Frankly, she felt as safe in a church as she did walking alone in the parking lot behind Sugar's Market to get to her car after work.

She and Hank had agreed to raise Letty in the church. After a proper baptism, they'd guiltily performed their rites only on Easter and Christmas and spoke fondly of the saints like they were cousins, lighting prayer candles all the time. But after

Hank's sudden death, and now the Hillbilly Hammer, Jane felt estranged from the church. Maybe a modicum closer to God.

Jane begged Hank to give her a sign that first year he was gone—anything, anything at all. A sign from him that she was doing a decent job raising their daughter, that he loved her still. If there was life beyond the living, beyond Sugar Bends, why wouldn't he give her a sign?

When Jane got home, she cut the engine in front of the old house, in the dirt patch she ambitiously called a yard. "Private Idaho" by The B-52's blared from Theo's work van, parked on the street.

"*Good, she's here.*" Jane approached Theo, who was hunched over the weeds. "Good afternoon," Jane said. Theo pushed her bifocals up with an index finger. "I want to thank you for helping my daughter last night."

"Sorry, the music." Theo shuffled for her phone in her cargo pocket, turning off the Bluetooth. "Say again?"

Jane noticed the lock screen on Theo's phone was a selfie of Nancy. She looked joyous, filled with life. Her eyes were a radiant green.

"Jesus wept," she said, briefly closing her eyes. "Would you join me inside?"

Lamplight filled the shotgun hallway, into the living room

and adjacent '70s rust-style brown and orange kitchen. Aluminum foil wallpapered the window glass. The curtains in the living room were drawn anyway, and the hand-me-down floral couch was covered in an afghan.

"It's untidy, like this uniform," Jane laughed sheepishly. "I don't get visitors. It's just me and my kid." She opened the refrigerator, taking out a pitcher of sweet tea. She poured some into a glass. "It's too hot for coffee. Tell me, your hair. How do you do that?"

"You need a lot of hands for braids. And a high pain tolerance."

The sink overflowed with dishes, and the linoleum counter space was crowded with cereal boxes and paper plates. Next to the sink was a ceramic bowl filled with candy corn.

"I wanted to thank you for taking care of my daughter last night," Jane said. "I'm a single mother and I can't always be front row for everything my daughter does."

"It's no trouble," Theo said, taking a sip of sweet tea. "Letty seems like a great kid."

Jane crossed her ankles, her fingers tracing the rim of the glass. "Theo, I know about your profession; while essential, it's gruesome. I know you were a first cleanup responder to Clint Ramirez and Christy Lyons's murders in January and March."

"Yes, I was there."

Jane's eyes flashed. "Letty's fond of you, she is. She's fascinated by your work. We're still coping with the loss of Hank. Letty's coping mechanisms are fine, for now. If she wants to think she can talk to the dead, sue me." She kicked off her Keds. Her brilliant red hair fell loose when she let her ponytail down. "I may wear a nametag, Theo, and don't you for one minute think I'm unappreciative of your line of work, but when I tell you Letty's impressionable . . . well, it's a lot to deal with. She's twelve. I don't want her knowing every brutality that's capable of happening on our streets."

Theo nodded. "You're on guard. I get it. I won't mention it to her again."

They drifted into the living room. Even with the warm lamplight, the house was still gloomy. The air conditioner ticked to life.

"Letty believes so fiercely she can hear her dad's presence. The less Letty hears about the dead, the better. Because when she grows out of this stage it's going to break her heart. And with the murders—Jesus help us."

"Who do you think is doing it?"

"A very evil person begging for mercy. I believe in forgiveness, but I also believe in justice. Nobody in this town knows a damn thing. I feel like the short order cook at the diner could catch this wretched man faster."

Jane sank into the couch. She sighed, wrinkling her face, looking twenty years older than she was. "The climate of this town is not merciful. My nerves are shot. And I don't just mean the Hillbilly Hammer murders, God knows. My windows barely lock and I can't afford new ones. I sure as heck can't afford a security camera. I don't even have a cell phone."

"Sugar Bends has a darkness about it," Theo said. "I'm a Scarecrow—I know you know what that is. I'm always keeping an eye on you and your kid."

Jane's worried frown twisted into confoundment and esteem. "Thank you, Theo. Scarecrow."

As she said the last word, Theo's phone lit up.

III

Theo grabbed her phone out of her pocket, excusing herself to the backyard with the wild sumac and dryer line. It would rain soon. *Unknown caller.* The voice introduced itself as Nolan Craven.

"This is Theo Shortridge. How can I help you today?"

"I need help with a cleanup. I've made a mess in my grief. Are you available?"

"I'm deeply sorry for your loss. I am available. Where are you located?"

"I'm south of Hounds in Sugar Bends, Florida. Do you know of it?"

"Absolutely. What type of death occurred, Mr. Craven?"

Theo glanced over her shoulder at Jane through the window. Her eyes looked like Letty's, cut out of the same cool rock. Theo resolved to watch over her and Letty, even harder than she'd already guarded them these last few months.

"It's too awful to talk about," Nolan said, his voice breaking. "I don't think I can."

Theo shivered from a brief gust coming down from the east. "I'm so sorry for your loss, Mr. Craven. Was this a violent death or a natural death? The more detail you give me, the more I can help you."

He sniffled and sighed, apologizing for his tears. "Forgive me," he said. "I've never felt like this before."

"That's quite alright, Mr. Craven." After a few moments, Theo asked again, "Do we have a natural death? A suicide? A homicide?"

Nolan sniffled. "Homicide. Kitchen."

Theo read off her privacy discretion and estimate. "And the police have ended their investigation, and the body is gone, correct?"

"Yes," Nolan cleared his throat. "The sheriff gave me your business card."

"Police have concluded that remediation is ready. I just need your address and we can make an appointment whenever you're ready."

Afterward, Theo thanked Jane for the company, who said from the porch step, "Come again, we're all God's children."

Across the street, a coyote hunched low on top of a steeply pitched roof stared at Theo.

IV

Sawyer flipped on 101.1 as he pulled out of the faculty parking lot and took off his necktie. The rain-induced heat trapped stale air in the Ford, and he put the windows down to savor the cleansing rain. Today's late-afternoon drive to the lighthouse felt particularly freeing after being corralled in a teacher's conference with Principal Barlow and Sheriff Baez. They were rolling out new safety guidelines for faculty and students that they'd postponed twice since the poor high school girl's death. (Miss Linda Carrigan spoke for thirty consecutive minutes.) Babes Henry had been his student once. She was a bright girl.

Sawyer disliked how Fischer Baez misspelled words in all the photocopied flyers posted around town, the ones he insisted on typing himself. The errors were all over town: the market, schools, post office, library. Everything was misspelled. Spellcheck was default on modern software. Something about that form of laziness in a grown man drove Sawyer up the wall.

My distinguished listeners, this is Tricia Cross. I want you to turn your hearts as high as they'll beat and help me honor the victims of the still-at-large Hillbilly Hammer.

Sawyer flipped on the windshield wipers as the temperature dropped and slashing rain made the Reduced Visibility sign foggy against the green and browned sugarcane fields.

These are the beautiful souls the Hillbilly Hammer has taken from us here in Sugar Bends: Clint Ramirez, rest in peace, January 21. Christy Lyons left us too soon on March 9. Phyllis Kratt, survived by four grandchildren, died on May 1. Trevor Winston, June 17. And, our innocence gutted, October 13, Margot "Babes" Henry. Take a minute.

Sawyer took a deep breath, pulling onto Griffin. Nancy Russo wasn't on the list. God, it had been nine months. He didn't want to show up to the lighthouse in a sour mood, but Tricia never honored Nancy's name. That upset Theo. Tricia did her dedications every other day, sometimes more, always leaving out Nancy.

"Where the hell are you, Nancy?" Sawyer said.

He'd been the leader of Nancy Russo's search party last winter, when everybody in town donned flashlights and went digging and yelling her name at Barrett's Woods, canoeing at Lake Briggs, and everywhere else all over town. After the searches, Theo quit showing up to Scarecrows meetings. She quit answering the phone. She didn't answer the door.

Let's hop right into The Allman Brothers Band, "Ain't Wastin' Time No More." Remember, folks, like the song says, time goes by like hurricanes and faster things. Let's make it count.

Faster things for sure, Sawyer thought, in Sugar Bends. Fast and cast to the darkness of this town. He flipped the radio off halfway through the song, parking down on Devil's Hill near some dogwood and palmettos. The petrichor was fresh as new soil, the rain quitting just long enough for him to gaze around the old campsite and make sure Fischer wasn't poking around. Could never be too careful. He hoped, and had reiterated to Tricia in bed the night before, that one year from now it would be him and Tricia and all their loving, no more hiding, no more cheating. They'd be together.

Sawyer was caught off guard by a man waving to him from the red buckeye in the brush. He had a handlebar mustache and wore a rawhide jacket. Looked like he was working there. Maybe a new caretaker.

"Good afternoon." The man waved, smiling. "Wet day, huh?"

He agreed. "Sure is."

Sawyer felt a grappling of electricity shoot through him first, that buzzing feeling like gentle fingers moving down a screen door. He instinctively grabbed his neck, wondering who the ghost in the fog was.

The man in the rawhide jacket with the round glasses

crossed the dirt path and headed toward the street on foot. Sawyer got back in the car and texted Tricia that he was on his way, but to lock the door until he arrived.

OCTOBER 27

I

It felt like fall for the first time Letty could remember. Sugar Bends looked just like Halloween in the movies, with crunchy leaves on the sidewalk and jack-o-lanterns aglow on porches. The air was crisp and chilly. For once, she wore a sweater all day. It was Friday after school, and the rest of the weekend was in front of her.

When the last school bell rang, Letty and Bernie rode their bikes past the library and laundromat to the Tidioute trailer park, deep in the pine-scrubbed woods. Tendrils of sunlight poured over the treetops.

"You got the *Magic: The Gathering* cards?" Bernie asked.

"At home. Mom was on my tail about getting to school on time. She was lecturing me about the buddy system, thanks to that stupid assembly."

"Crap. Maybe we should just walk and spy."

The girls hopped off their bikes. They could hear lizards scuttle into storm drains moored above driftwood. A group of high school kids sat on top of a Dodge drinking Pabst, talking in low voices amongst themselves.

"Joe snatched ten dollars out of my fair-ticket money for gas. I'm telling mom 'cuz that's some bullshit. He thinks he can rat on me because he knows we go to the cemetery every day," Bernie said.

Joe was Bernie's sixteen-year-old brother. He ran track. He worked serving hamburgers at the Dairy Queen in Hounds.

"Told you, Bern, even if the Halloween fair happens, no way our moms will let us go."

Bernie was one of the few kids in Sugar Bends whose parents were still married. It made her sort of special. Her mom, Kat, worked in a nail salon. Her dad, Mike, was a grocer. Letty liked to eat dinner with the Acosta's on Saturdays when her mom was at work, and pretend she was one of them. A big family like that, it was kind of fun to pretend to be a part of the group.

"Your mom and dad are still letting Joe go to work?" Letty asked.

"For now. He's gotta help pay for his shit-ass self, serial killer or not."

Police sirens squalled in the distance. One of the teenagers on the Dodge, now behind the girls, started hollering.

"This way. Cops are ready to snatch kids up nowadays," Letty said.

They turned left toward two trailers stacked side by side, with cats in the yard. The smell of wet pine was in the air. It had been a sweltering summer; this was the first crisp, cool day.

"Real talk: Shuri or Black Widow?" Bernie asked.

Letty picked up a rock under the staggerbush, throwing it as hard as she could. "Shuri. She's the real Black Panther and stronger than Widow."

"What if they were fighting each other?" Bernie said.

"Shuri, still. No question. She wins all further technical questions."

"You and your technical BS." Bernie crushed a Grit beer can with her sneaker. Her shoelaces were filthy. "Did you hear that Everett Myers went out with Babes Henry one time?"

"I thought it was Lisle Baruso."

"Nah, Joe told me. His dumb girlfriend, Phoebe, dated Everett."

"Everett's such a loser."

"So is she."

Letty had to laugh, even if it was true. Phoebe and Everett were made for each other, both equally irritating. Phoebe Saxon and Joe Acosta had been dating for six months, which seemed like an eternity to her.

More teenagers showed up around a cluster of mangroves

near a double-wide trailer, drinking beer.

"Do you want to play Light as a Feather, Stiff as a Board?"

"We're not kids anymore. I don't think so."

"Kids don't levitate," Letty said, matter-of-factly.

Letty's eyes roved the woods. There were more kids out then she thought, certainly more of the big teenagers that seemed four times their size. "You know what I've been thinking? Why was Margot's nickname Babes?"

"The other girls gave her that nickname."

"Doesn't seem feminist, to me. But who cares, she's dead now. It's no wonder she was murdered by a bad guy. That's what happens to girls like Babes when they've got a lot of friends, or even if they don't."

"You're messed up, Letty. She was just popular."

Letty nudged Bernie, shushing her at the sight of somebody between two double-wide trailers in the distance.

"Get down," she said. They hid behind a sumac bush, their knees in a patch of dirt. The trailer adjacent to the RV and tarped generator was where the satanic orgies went on, Letty was sure of it.

"Think he's the killer?" Bernie whispered.

"I wonder if the police have looked in that RV."

"Let's go 'round the side."

Letty was excited for adventure. Bernie hadn't been into spying as much as she used to, but this felt like a real game. They waited until the man, Ben Ashcroft—the guy that owned the gas station—turned around, and they crab-walked toward the RV, ducking behind its tires.

Ben dragged a lawn chair from a tool shed alongside his white-shingled trailer, placed it next to an acoustic granddaddy guitar, and sat down.

"He's a Scarecrow, that guy," Letty whispered.

The man turned his face toward the treetops. He wore flannel and blue jeans.

"See if the RV's unlocked," Bernie said, shooing Letty toward the door with her free hand. "Go 'head."

"I'm always the one doing the work around here."

Ben couldn't see them from his lawn chair. The RV was to the left of where he strummed that guitar in simple C and E slides. Letty waited a minute and then took three steps toward the RV, where she scurried up to its door. She was afraid an alarm was going to blast. Surely a cop was lurking behind a tree.

"Go," Bernie shooed again.

"Hold your horses," Letty said.

Letty unlatched the RV's door, mentally tallying the most irresponsible things she and Bernie had ever done at the park.

The door opened. It was so dark that Letty blinked, willing her eyes to adjust. He could be it. He could be The Hillbilly Hammer.

"Are there bodies? Dead ones?" Bernie said.

Letty didn't answer. The orgies! People's gross bodies entangled with one another, sweating and making animal sounds, she was sure to walk in on it. "Shit," she said. She returned her gaze back to the RV and the man, and the Scarecrow playing guitar on his own property stood before her with his arms crossed. "Oh—Hello."

"Hello, girls. What do you need this time?"

"This time?" Bernie said.

"You girls were here a few weeks ago standing on my pop crates looking through my window. Made my beagle, Hijinx, lose his lunch. That's right, girls, I know what you're doing, and I'd appreciate it if you'd stop." Ben tried not to smile; Letty could see that much. He was skinnier up close.

"We did that?" Letty said. "I don't think so."

Letty's face turned red.

"Selective memory is a common disease. My name is Ben Ashcroft."

Bernie scampered away from Ben and pulled Letty with her, apologizing faster than they ever had in their lives. They were tripping over themselves as they ran off into the woods.

Letty and Bernie ran all the way to Pennecamp Road, past the beer-drinking teens on top of the Dodge and the other trailers. When they got to the road, they realized they didn't have their bikes. Letty bent down to catch her breath.

"What the hell do we do now?" Bernie said. "My mom's gonna kill me if I tell her I lost my bike!"

"You didn't lose it, you know where it is," Letty said. "It's right by Ben Ashcroft's place. We can go back and get it later."

"Freakin' great."

"Think he's the killer?" Letty said.

"I think I want my bike back."

The girls picked up their pace, moaning about the long walk home.

"What's wrong with you?" Letty said. "Why do you look like that?"

"Because I'm pissed, that's why! Letty, everything's always your fault! This stupid spying and looking for the killer and talking to the dead! Well, now we don't have our bikes and don't know how we're gonna get them back!"

Letty stopped in her tracks. "I'll go get them, if you're gonna act like that."

"No, you won't. Your mom's gonna be home soon and

there's a curfew. We're not even supposed to be out right now. We get caught, we're in even more trouble. And my mom's gonna know I don't have my bike because I ride to school—you know that. This really bites my ass."

"Fine then, if you didn't want to come, you should've followed curfew. Be a little rule follower!"

Bernie scowled. "And I'm not going back to the cemetery again. So, screw you."

"Fine, nobody asked you to!"

"Good!"

"Talking Dead Society sucks anyway," Bernie said. "There, I said it."

"Talking Dead Society's over."

In that moment, Letty knew things had changed, and not just in the ways of avoiding the Timbers, going to school, or biking until sundown. Sugar Bends—their town, their home—was grappling with murders, and the constant fear changed everybody and everything they'd once known. Bernie was angry. There was a bad man in the places they used to play.

II

en Ashcroft strummed, the sweet and soft sounds of his guitar filling the air. His '92 Gibson was his favorite thing he owned, next to Hijinx, of course, the old mutt. Ben had lived in Florida long enough to know when to enjoy a cool, brisk afternoon, one of those rare times when morning felt like it could last all day.

He looked up into the treetops, knowing someone—or something—dark was watching the town.

The Hillbilly Hammer was legally known as Nolan Craven, but Ben had no way to prove it, especially when the man in question was dead and buried after the 1988 winter fire at the mill. He'd seen the guy around over the years, blending in with the town, observant and organized, transient. Nolan Craven had succeeded at seeming semi-human.

Nolan went from being an antisocial personality—living in a cracker house on Loxahatchee Road, working at the mill, single—to something unremorseful and evil.

Ben peered up above him through the treetops, thinking of the Scarecrows. Tricia Cross, Roberta Quentin, Sawyer Harris, and goddamn it, Theo Shortridge. He needed them all to stop the Hillbilly Hammer, to make some sense of it.

The wind regathered its original cold punch, shrieking like a train whistle. He laid the guitar next to him in the grass. His eyes roved the property. Next door, a double-wide trailer was quiet. The girls were long gone, their bikes left next to his RV. He inhaled the sweet turpentine, walking into the woods. Hijinx barked while following at his old man's ankles.

"You out there, Nolan? I know you're listening," Ben said. "I'm not afraid of you. You've made your point. I don't know what you want here, but your games are over. You're getting old inside—you should be an old man now. Time to retire."

The sunlight threaded through the woods. It felt like January in the shade. Ben walked back to the trailer and grabbed his phone.

"Roberta, I think we need a meeting tomorrow."

Sugar Bends was feeling strange again.

III

Everett Myers drove his just-waxed Corvette fifty miles per hour in a thirty-five, wearing a goblin-green mask with a black hood, arm pumping in the air as Lisle Baruso hung his head out the window like a golden retriever. Lisle waved a baseball bat, howling vulgarities to people on the sidewalk, as J.T. Alvarez and Brent Lowe erupted into laughter in the backseat.

They drove along Lake Briggs, farting around just long enough for Everett to flip on 101.1.

"Let's go scare that radio bitch," Everett said.

J.T. tinkered on his phone. "Our park bender last week almost got us in the slammer, yo."

"*Yo*, it *did* get us in the slammer; was nothing—noth*ing*. We're just gonna scare her, we aren't gonna do nothing," Lisle said. "Maybe we can get her screeching her lungs out on air."

"Yeah, lighten up, man," Brent said.

Good afternoon, Sugar Bends; or, if you're just waking up, good day, sleepy head, and welcome to 101.1, where it's Friday and Halloween's around the corner. I've heard through the tumultuous grapevine that Halloween's banned this year in Sugar Bends. So put your spooky masks on and sit on your front porch with a beer and some candy corn, because this is as good as it's gonna get.

"Tricia can slob my knob with a mask on or off," Everett said.

"We're coming to get you, Tricia!" Lisle said. He shot a dirty look at Everett. "You look a goddamn goon with that mask on. Take that off."

"No chance. I'm gonna scare the living hell out of that bitch."

"What did she ever do to you?" J.T. said. "Tricia's hot."

Lake Briggs gleamed smooth in the sun, surrounded by tightly packed mangroves and laurel oaks with Spanish moss. When they got to Devil's Hill, they parked down by the driftwood. Nobody else was around, not even the caretaker. The lighthouse was just down the path, up the hill, and up the stairs.

Tricia Cross was one of them Scarecrow freaks. For reasons Everett didn't know, that pissed him off. The Scarecrows were stupid people. They thought they were all high and mighty. His dad said they didn't pay taxes.

"Tricia was a real slut back in the day," J.T. said.

"She's a MILF now," Brent said, throwing his cigarette butt out of the car window. "I'm fine with that."

Everett parked the Corvette by a laurel oak, canopied by

Spanish-moss. The boys jumped out of the car and hit the pathway up the hill toward the No Trespassing sign marked in yellow. Everett reminded them of the plan. The plan was to climb the stairs and knock on the lighthouse door a few times, then wait for Tricia to investigate the noise. While her back was turned, they'd hustle up the stairs and hide somewhere near the bay windows. Jump out, scare the living shit out of her. Maybe do it while she was on air and get her reaction over the radio.

"Hold it, I left my mask back at the Corvette," Everett said.

"Why the hell did you take it off?" Lisle said.

"Never mind. I'll meet you at the stairs. Hurry up and don't let anybody see you."

Everett, a flop of blond hair in his face, jogged back to the Corvette. He reached into the passenger side window for the goblin-green mask. He pulled the hood on and adjusted the stretched, ugly goblin face. He checked himself in the side mirror. A man was standing behind him.

Everett gasped.

"Shit," he said, losing his balance.

"I need a favor," the man said through bared teeth.

Everett felt a titanium hammer crunch into his face. His eye popped out of its socket, and for a moment, he could feel it hanging wetly by his broken cheekbone. Lots of weight to it, bloody. He felt blood. He could taste blood. He felt abnormally hot. Then, he realized what happened, and he couldn't talk, couldn't make a sound. The hammer came down again and he saw the man that delivered the blow, long black hair and the blackest eyes. Then, only darkness.

IV

Theo's driving music on the way to Nolan Craven's house was "Ask the Angels." She loved playing Patti Smith at maximum volume. It felt like true autumn. She could smell pine. She caught herself smiling in the rearview mirror on the drive, and it made her feel like a traitor, almost obscene. She couldn't remember the last time she looked at herself in the mirror and smiled. Weeks of anxiety had aged her, and now she only bore a strong resemblance to the woman she used to be before Nancy disappeared. If she died of a broken heart, what would the coroner think was the cause? Undiagnosed heart disease? Accidental overdose?

Theo drove south on River Cross where The Bends shopping mall used to be. She remembered a music store there called Spinner's that she'd spent all her weekends in, eons ago, in the '90s. The only business that still thrived on that side of town was the only funeral parlor in Sugar Bends. She got to Cinder Street and parked on the street. This house looked like hers, with a Florida room sticking out the front, stones stilting the sea green wood frame, and a concrete chimney. The backyard was separated by a chain-link fence. Theo could smell the squalor from her truck.

"Christ," she said. She put on a new respirator, grabbed a clipboard, and cut the engine. There were anthills between blades of crabgrass. She noticed fire ants zeroing in on a window trellis. Nolan greeted her at the door.

"Thank you for coming on such short notice," Nolan said. He stepped to the side to let Theo in. The smell was putrid, exactly what a corpse rotting in the July sun would smell like. A blow of hot air escaped the room, puffing Theo's cheeks from the heat, even from underneath the respirator.

"I'm Theo Shortridge, your cleanup technician. It's nice to meet you, Mr. Craven."

"Please, call me Nolan."

The man was emotionally bereft, that much was certain. Bleary bags under his eyes indicated he hadn't slept in days. His long black hair looked unwashed. It was typical to see a client's post-death behavior aligned with hoarding or depression; sometimes the client was so apologetic it was hard to get work done. This man was no different.

"May I see the room where—"

"I'm struck by your grief. I can feel it coming off you like stovetop heat," Nolan said, shutting the door. He wore a rawhide jacket and blue jeans. There was a darker shade of blue patched on his knee.

"Excuse me?"

Nolan gently extended his hand, as if to touch an invisible line. "Forgive me, it's just— you've suffered a significant loss."

Theo cocked her head, looking into the small marbles of his eyes, which she could see underneath his big glasses. "I'd say lucky guess, Nolan, but it sounds like we're going through the same thing."

"You always think your parents will live forever."

"I'm deeply sorry for your loss."

The wooden floor creaked under Theo's feet. She waddled in the ballooning hazard suit as she walked down the shotgun hallway, eyes roving. There were only a few armchairs and a TV. "Tell me, Nolan, what made you think I've suffered a loss?"

"I told you—like stovetop heat," Nolan's voice dropped a pitch.

Theo noticed the change as she pulled on rubber gloves. The squalid smell, which had been bitter and expired, evaporated. All at once, she couldn't sense the polluted air.

"I cleaned up everything before you arrived," Nolan said. "It was the least I could do. One last favor for Mother."

Theo turned sharply to face him. "What?"

"One last favor for Mother. Favors are what make a

community, or even a small town like this one, Sugar Bends."

"You've remediated the cleanup yourself. Will you still need my cleaning services?"

"Yes."

Theo clenched her fist nervously. "Where did the homicide occur?"

"You're standing in the room. It was here, among the kitchen things."

Theo thought about her supply cart she left in the work van: biohazard bags, deodorizer, disinfectant, bleach, scraper, gloves, the works. Guess she'd roll the supply cart in and get to work. "I'll have to take pictures of the cleanup you conducted, Mr. Craven, and then I can begin a deep clean of the kitchen."

Nolan smiled thinly, colorless eyes burning right through those lenses. Theo looked away instinctively. The kitchen was spotless except for aged linoleum and countertops.

"Are you alright, Mrs. Shortridge?"

"Where did you . . . dispose of the soiled wreckage?"

"That's what I wanted to talk to you about, Mrs. Shortridge. I know we've only just met, but I'm in need of a favor."

Theo drew a sigh, feeling a rise in her chest. "What's going on?"

"I've lived here my whole long, long life. But this is just one small town for me, among many I've been to. The satisfaction of having a neighbor means there's always somebody to lend a favor. Can you do me a favor?"

"I don't—"

Nolan stepped forward. His boots were silent on the wooden floor. "You did a phenomenal job cleaning up the school shooting in Hounds last year. That was really something that shook the town, wasn't it? Almost as bad as the Hillbilly Hammer—worse, really, what with children and all. I think cleaning up that kind of trauma means you have resolute willpower."

"Who told you I was involved with that high school?"

"The sheriff. I coaxed it out of him, really. It wasn't my business, but I'm old-fashioned. It was you and fifteen other crime-techs from out of state—Louisiana, to be precise— working twenty-nine hours to scrub lockers and desks. Must've been brutal to see."

"It was," Theo said.

"I'm sorry for beating around the bush. The favor is about the wreckage I cleaned up here today, a few hours before you arrived. The cleanup job I have in mind fits your trauma criteria, and it's not nearly as bad as what was here this morning: blood, mostly blood. I used washcloths and bed linens to clean. Nearly bruised dents in my hand."

Nolan held up his hands. His palms were calloused pink.

He continued, "There's a place called The Pits on the edge of town. It's an abandoned rest stop facing Mayday Motel near the mill. Nothing you haven't seen before, this place, just rags and linens. I threw the trash bags in the utility room to get them out of my sight. I couldn't bear to throw Mother away like that. There's—" Nolan sniffled, dropping his chin. His eyes swelled with tears. He flipped his long hair out of his face. "Sorry."

"Nolan—"

"It's just the police, they wouldn't *help me* clean up . . . the horrible fragments of bones. Bones, Theo, *bones*. No child should have to clean up their parents' bones."

Theo dropped her gaze to the floor as he sobbed. How the hell long had he kept his mother in the house? "It's true. There's not a lot of remediation support for families, even in the most gruesome of situations. I thought you said this was a homicide." She knew then it must have been gunshots, had to be a shotgun. Something that would literally blow the head or limb off somebody.

"I wanted to clean up Mother *for* Mother, but I couldn't put it in the dump like I wanted to. I couldn't bear it." He paused, locking eyes with her. "Could you do me that favor?"

"Listen, Nolan, what I can do for you—"

Nolan's cryptic expression returned. "I'll bring back Nancy."

Suddenly, a yellow film veiled Theo's vision. She heard a fizzling and then a snap. Everything was sunflower-bright. She felt wonderful. She felt rested and full of happiness, even love. Nancy was alive. Nancy stood in front of her, sharp but helplessly giggly and sweet-faced. Not a scar marked her, not a single fright had ever graced that smiling face. It didn't feel real, to be that high on love.

Theo jolted back to the grim, standstill reality of standing in her hazard suit in this stranger's house. She gasped. The dream was over.

"Nancy," Theo cried. "But she was just here—"

"That's right," Nolan said. "I'll bring Nancy back from the dead. She will be like you remember her."

A pummel of dizziness flooded Theo. She gulped. "Where's Nancy? Is she alright?"

"I'm afraid not. But I've accessed those gray areas in towns like this, and I can bring her back just like you remember her. No more splitting headaches, panic attacks, or crying jags. I can bring her back and your grief will lift."

Theo shook her head. A lick of sweat dripped down her back. She dropped the clipboard and took off the respirator. Strands of braids fell from their clipped-in position in the back of her head. "Listen, asshole—"

"Watch."

Nolan gestured to the JAM tattoo on Theo's knuckles. The black-inked letters bubbled up out of her skin, turning into a different word. It felt like a coal burn. The word NANCY appeared, one letter for each finger. Theo screamed, falling to the floor.

"Look again."

JAM had returned, the burning faded, and her hand was hers again. "Who the fuck are you? You're just a . . . a trick!"

Nolan frowned, keeping his distance from Theo as she flipped her hand over, examining her fingers, examining her other hand. "I owe you an apology, Theo. I'm sorry. See? I'm crying too."

"You're fucking crying. What the *fuck* do you want?" She got to her feet.

"Please. I have a gift, and it is not unlike your gift, but it is different and must be used sparingly. I simply want you to drive to The Pits."

Theo didn't want to piss him off. She wanted whatever this

was to end. The sharpest accessory she had on her was the van's keys. But she couldn't move. "It's a rest stop."

"I've put Mother's things in the utility room. Nothing gruesome, like I explained. There won't be any surprises. But I couldn't dispose of the things myself. I never was taught when to ask for help. You see, her bones . . . there's fragments of her bones in the linen sheets and I just want them disposed of. I'm sorry to ask you this way, but you hesitated."

"You're fucking insane."

"I can't resuscitate old souls. I've tried, and I can't."

"But you can bring her back to me? How the hell are you going to do that?"

"I felt your grief. I was burned in a fire. Heat isn't lost on me. I feel it all the time, even from far away. Grief is no different. I have so much oxygen flowing through me, enough to restore her back to you, back to your home."

Theo froze. She studied his brooding face, that mustache. Her mind raced as he lifted his eyeglass lenses, that colorless stare seeping into her.

"If you try and rape me, I'll cut your dick off. I'll kill you."

"You have my word. I haven't been mechanical there in years. I'm not advancing violence. Isn't that a coping mechanism for grief, helping others? This is a favor, it's just a favor."

"What are you?"

Nolan looked out the window. "The sun's beginning to set. That chill from earlier was so welcoming."

"I'm gonna ask again: what are you? And what are you doing here?"

"Born intuitive, burned gifted."

Theo charged for the door. She didn't have a plan.

Nolan said, "Theodora Jessie Shortridge attended community college in Hounds, didn't graduate. Only child to Robin and Michael. Long-time motorcyclist. You have sour milk in your fridge that needs tossing before garbage day. Your wife, Nancy Russo, whom you met in high school, has been missing since December 28 of last year."

With her hand on the doorknob, Theo turned back to face Nolan again. His shoulders were slumped, and he frowned. She noticed his boots, soiled with sand.

"I've picked up on all of that since you walked into this house."

"Congratulations, you're an organized stalker. I'm getting the sheriff, and don't you fucking come near me when I walk out this door."

The lock on the door clicked in her palm.

"I really tried being considerate that time," Nolan said. "You go to The Pits the day after tomorrow, or you live as long as I've lived in all-consuming, all-suffering, deep, ambushed grief. And you never see your wife again. Your memories will fade, but you won't know why. You won't know why you feel so sad. Don't get anybody involved. Don't make it harder on yourself. We both know you've got nothing to lose."

Theo, filled with stark terror, stifled a cry. "What if I say no?"

"Clean up what you see, and I'll bring her back to you. Your grief will be forgotten. Life will be as it once was. Remember: born intuitive, burned gifted."

The lock unclicked in her hand, and she fled down the concrete steps and into the work van, wondering if this was equivalent to selling her soul, and if it were, it would be worth it. God, it would be worth it.

OCTOBER 28

I

espite a heated meeting at town hall, which included Placerville's Women's Club and the PTA raising hell, the annual Halloween fair was going on as scheduled. It was the forty-third year for Sugar Bends, and for three nights the police agreed to lift the curfew. Give the people some normalcy, folks argued. Do it for the kids.

The first year of the fair, back in the early 1970s, started as a fall festival. Herman's Hermits came to sing. Mr. Sparky Sumpter, who now had a plaque in the park dedicated to him, won the state record for growing the largest corn stalk. Since then, the fair's corn maze was the most anticipated attraction and tradition, decorated with hay and carved pumpkins to look like autumn in Salem, Massachusetts.

Letty had ideas. Jane was a stickler for having Letty home by dark, but on the first night of the fair, she was working a double shift at the diner. She wouldn't be home until morning, and Letty reasoned that what her mother didn't know couldn't kill her, or even worry her.

It had gotten dark early when Letty, Bernie, and Cameron

hiked all the way to the fair, the sky a toasted golden brown.

"I know what my costume is gonna be," Bernie said. She and Letty hadn't so much as glanced at each other since yesterday's argument. They crossed McClellan, jaunting along dense pine scrub where few canopied trees provided shade, and the prairie was straight ahead. "I'm going as Shuri, the real Black Panther."

"Real shocker," Cameron said.

"I know mine," Letty said. "David Bowie, the singer guy. I saw a wig at the hardware store."

Bernie scoffed. "But your hair's too long."

"I can do the lightning bolt makeup," Cameron said. "I'm getting swell at it. Just don't let your face get in the way of my work."

"What are you going as, Cam?" Bernie said.

Cars whined past them as the fair came into view. The fenced-off parking area was just ahead. "Ghostface from *Scream*."

"Don't you think that's insensitive?" Letty snapped. "All these murders around town?"

"Not as insensitive as all the kids that are gonna go as the Hillbilly Hammer."

"He's got a point," Bernie said. "I heard Brick Myers was

doing that one."

The fairground shimmered in neon lights. Teenagers roamed in packs, smoking cigarettes, glaring at younger kids having fun. There were five rides and one merry-go-round. The rides spun, dropped, and twirled like pendulums. Letty, Bernie, and Cameron couldn't help but comment on Babes Henry, how she'd come here with friends last year on a night like tonight, riding rides and playing ring toss. Now she was dead.

They were giddy on Ghost Coaster, shrieking to their hearts content as the vehicle plunged down a track into a wallpapered, scrimmed mine. House of Mirrors was a hoot, too. Letty and Bernie forgot all about their argument and the bikes they lost in Mr. Ashcroft's yard. Soon, they were laughing and pushing through purple-lit corridors, each narrower than the last. They were so rambunctious and giggly that the operator outside told them to cut it out.

On the exit ramp at the merry-go-round, Cameron gestured toward a crowd forming at the hotdog stall. A fight was breaking out. A teenager had punched another teenager. It looked like one of the Timbers. "Did you see that right hook slam?" he said. "I think that's J.T. what's-his-name."

"Come on, let's skedaddle," Bernie said.

At the entrance to the corn maze, Brick the Dick stood with his friends, wearing a ski mask, holding a toy hatchet. Full dick crew tonight.

"Oh, look, it's Brick the Dick," Letty said. "Police said no masks, no costumes."

"Then why'd they let you in, freak?" Brick retorted. "Corn maze is closed, girls." He leaned coolly over a hedge of hay, a total twin of his older brother.

Letty rolled her eyes as they skirted past Brick the Dick and his friends. She hoped Brick saw her roll her eyes. She wanted him to know how dumb and rude she thought he was. Letty, Bernie, and Cameron made three wrong turns in the corn maze, eventually walking down a sloped path with bundled hay stacked around cotton scarecrows with straw hats. Five minutes in, and they were already lost.

The straw path narrowed. Hay bale hedges and plastic pumpkins surrounded Brick the Dick and the rest of the Timbers: Lisle Baruso, J.T. Alvarez, and Brent Lowe, minus Brick's brother, Everett. Brick the Dick hitched his comb-over out from the ski mask holes, raising his toy hatchet at the friends.

"Like I'm really scared," Letty said. "Why don't you get a life?"

When the friends turned their backs, Brick the Dick threw the hatchet in their direction. "Made you flinch," he said. "Can me and my friends here get some help through this corn maze? We're lost."

"*Get* lost," Letty said.

"He's fucking with us," Bernie said.

"Dream on, boy scout," Cameron said.

Brick the Dick trailed behind the three of them, throwing popcorn and whipping insults the whole way, the hedges brushing their legs.

"Bernadette," Brick the Dick called. "Will you help me take my wang out of my pants so I can piss?"

"Still obsessed with penis," Bernie said. "Why don't you leave us the hell alone?"

"Yeah, where's your asinine brother anyway?" Cameron asked.

Brick the Dick shrugged. "He does whatever he wants."

"We don't know where Everett's at," Lisle said, nudging J.T. "Last we saw Everett was when we were at the car together. We thought he'd meet us here if nothing else."

Brent spit, lighting a cigarette. "You sound like my mother, man. He's probably getting some from Tricia Cross."

"You shouldn't talk about girls that way," Letty said,

looking over her shoulder at the bullies.

"Keep talking like that you're gonna wind up like Babes Henry, six feet under," Lisle said.

Other high school and middle school kids skirted by, avoiding the confrontation. The three of them arrived at the maze's exit, picking up the pace. They dodged being seen by the Timbers kneeling behind a popcorn and pretzel cart, crawling on their hands and knees up a patch of grass to the merry-go-round. It was hot. And the heat combined with the grinning scarecrows and stacked pumpkins were a special cloying nostalgia for the friends.

On the way to the Ferris wheel, Letty thought, *nobody understands me.* Sometimes it just felt like Bernie was the brave one, and Cameron the smart one. Bernie hadn't wanted to do much spying anymore, and Talking Dead Society was pretty much over. Letty watched Bernie and Cameron shoot the shit on the way up the ramp.

They got in line at the loading platform. A dirge melody played, and below them, kids shouted at the pow-wow and whirly games.

"Sorry, miss, you'll have to wait your turn," the attendant said. Letty waved to her friends.

"See you at the top!" Cameron said.

Letty thought it might be nice to ride by herself. But when she got in the compartment, a man joined her as the lap bar came down.

The dirge melody got louder as the cable car lifted. The neon lights from Ghost Coaster turned a shade of orange from off in the distance, lighting up the prairie.

"I forgot my manners. My name's Nolan Craven."

Letty didn't want to be rude either. "Letty."

"Letty, nice to meet you."

It was weird being alone with a grown, male stranger. He wore a suede-type jacket with fringe on the pockets, the color of cowboy leather. You didn't see too many men with long hair. It seemed like something from her dad's time, or even older than that. She looked toward the lighthouse off Devil's Hill, the surrounding woods beyond the prairie line illuminated with a warm glow.

On the final lift, Nolan smiled as the revolving car glided up. They were almost to the top. "I'm sorry about your father, Letty Hardin."

Letty froze. She firmly clenched the lap bar.

"Sorry, my manners again. I used to work with your father, Hank, before the pandemic. We worked together at the sugarcane mill. You probably don't remember me."

Letty let out a sigh of relief. She thought he was a creeper at first, but it was just a guy that knew her dad. She'd met quite a few of them over the years, ran into them at Sugar's Market, at the post office. She felt like she was being rude.

"No, actually," she stammered, "I do remember you."

"I sometimes see you and your mother in line at Sugar's," Nolan said. "I'm the doofy guy buying all the snacks, all the stuff my doctor says I shouldn't put in my shopping cart."

Letty chuckled. She searched her mind. Nolan Craven. She supposed she had seen this man before. Old people all looked the same.

"Say," Nolan began, "your dad was a great man. I loved working with him. I lost my mother recently. It doesn't matter how old you are, you need your parents."

"Yeah," Letty agreed. She wanted off the ride now. He seemed nice enough, but she realized she'd forgotten the pepper spray again. *Lighten up, Letty*, she thought to herself. *This is why Bernie and Cam think you're a little kid.*

The mechanics of the Ferris wheel went into high gear, and the descent began as the music played on.

"Can I ask you a favor, Letty Hardin?" His demeanor changed. Letty, breathless, saw Nolan Craven strangely loom over her like a tower, bending into the sky. He turned giant-like. She realized that she'd seen him before, in the fields across from the gas station after school.

Suddenly, he was back to normal—unflappable and soft-spoken.

Nolan said, "I love small towns because you can depend on people. Can I depend on you for something?"

"I'm not—"

"If you tell me everything you know about Theo Shortridge—*Theo Shortridge*—I promise you'll hear from your father again. You talk to the dead, don't you?"

"How do you know that?"

"When my mother died, God rest her soul, my sadness turned into something else. I can feel things, Letty, like you can. I'm an old man capable of many things. I know it's been a long, long time since you've felt your father. You're forgetting his voice."

Letty's guts churned. She hadn't told anybody that, not her mother, not Bernie, and not her therapist, Mrs. Sanders. She gulped, feeling her cheeks get hot. "I don't want to forget his voice."

"Of course not. I don't want to forget my mother's voice, either. Tell me about Theo Shortridge and you will hear his voice again. You will feel him all around you." Nolan lifted the lenses on his big, round eyeglasses. His eyes flickered black. The smell of smoke snuck into Letty's nose.

She let go of the lap bar. Black confetti fell out of her palms, sprinkling her lap and the floor of the cable car. She gasped. "Who are you? What's happening?"

"I tried saving your father when he collapsed. He told me to tell you he loved you. I can get him back to you, in special ways, psychic ways. The ways you've practiced with your friends. But you must do me this one favor."

Letty's eyes filled with tears. Her father loved her. He was still out there, loving her, watching her, and she was the last thing he thought of before he died. Letty wiped her nose on her sleeve. On the descent, she told Nolan that Theo Shortridge cleaned up trauma scenes. She'd been married to a woman named Nancy, but Nancy disappeared last year, and nobody has seen her since. Nolan asked Letty to tell him what he didn't know.

"Theo," Letty said. "She's my neighbor. She lives at 417 Loxahatchee Rd. She's nice."

"Your neighbor?" Nolan said. "Really?"

"You're looking for her?"

Nolan smiled as the ride came to a complete stop. "I sure have been. For a long time."

"Mister, Nolan, when will I hear from my dad?"

"Very soon. Be seeing you, Letty Hardin."

Letty went to find her friends. She couldn't wait to get home.

II

The Chevy got its makeover. New battery, oil change, oiled brakes, new transmission, two new tires, and Josiah insisted on a wash and wax. Unfortunately, Angie's brightened mood didn't last when night came; it was time to retrieve that dead girl's headstone.

"It's darker out here than that time in Broken Arrow after the mudslide. We played Tanya Tucker and drank moonshine all night, 'member that? Joey?" Angie sighed irritably, sitting on the passenger side. "You're not listening."

Josiah didn't answer. Angie sighed again, hoping he'd hear her loud and clear. They'd left their motel room half past midnight. There was some Halloween to-do on the other side of town, and she begged Josiah to go, just to get a glimpse of the Ferris wheel and maybe some cotton candy. Maybe they could spend a few hours and he could win her a teddy bear to sit on the dash.

Of course, they had other obligations.

Josiah made a sharp turn off Sheridan Street, nearly hitting the guardrail by a pawn shop.

"Slow down, Joey! You remember what Nolan said. Don't draw no attention."

"Okay, Angie, I saw it!"

"You're yelling at me, Joey!"

"I'm thinkin' is all! I'm sorry, baby." Josiah slowed down to thirty. "It shouldn't be much farther. We get the shovels and shit, then hit up the cemetery. And no fooling around." He shot Angie a glance. "No stupid Halloween kid shit. We've got work to do."

Angie groaned, looking out the window at the cracker houses. It wasn't fair. She just wanted a couple hours of enjoyment. Josiah never liked to do anything fun. Her curls blew in front of her face. "We're doing this for the money, right?"

Josiah finally smiled. "Money, baby. Think about that farmhouse. Soon the only place we'll be running to is the hospital so you can have the baby. Then we'll come home, sip some beers on the porch swing, rock the little girl to sleep."

"You think it'll be a girl?"

"Yeah, I sure do."

Angie agreed it was going to be a girl. She crossed her arms in her bomber jacket. It was her favorite piece of clothing she owned. She got it at Goodwill and had sewn three silver studs above the breast pocket. Even when it was hot, she wore the thing. It was comforting, something she'd bought for herself.

Moonlight fluttered across the hood of the Chevy as they drove along the tallgrass prairie where nothing but cabbage and electric pylons grew for half a mile.

"Taking this headstone gives me the creeps. What do you think Nolan's gonna do to my daddy?"

"Give him a taste of his own medicine," Josiah said, not taking his eyes off the road.

An announcement came over the radio and Angie turned it up.

Distinguished listeners, if you're just tuning in, this is 101.1 and I'm Tricia Cross. Police are currently combing the scene outside Devil's Hill, north of Lake Briggs, where—I'm sorry to report—a young man, Everett Myers, a senior at Earl Jones High School—was found murdered, bludgeoned with that goddamn hammer. I-I-I don't want to read this next part. Give me a minute.

"Joey, what's she talking about?" Angie said.

That poor boy, Everett Myers, his head is . . . missing. Authorities are searching for the decapitated . . . head at the scene. If you know any information, you're encouraged to call the station immediately. More details as we have them. Police will hold a conference at 8:00 a.m. tomorrow morning, and it will be televised locally. This is the sixth murder under the Hillbilly Hammer. God help us. Stay safe out there, Sugar Bends. Stay safe.

"Another murder?" Angie said. "What the fuck is going on?"

"I don't know."

Angie flicked the radio off. She didn't want to hear anymore. Her eyes blazed. "Decapitated. That Nolan guy did that, and me and you are the only ones that know."

"Killer or not, he's all we got right now, and we got a favor to do so we can get the hell out of this town."

Angie noticed Josiah's fear. She'd never seen him scared before. Not like this. Not with a clenched jaw and sweat beading down the back of his neck.

They arrived at The Pits. The overgrown weeds and tall pine scrub were so thick, you'd almost miss the rest stop if you weren't trying. No floodlights either.

"We'll never see where we're stepping," Angie said.

They left the Chevy running, with the high beams turned on. The picnic tables were graffitied, and beer cans littered the crabgrass that stank from baking in the sun. MEN to the left, WOMEN to the right, and down the middle was a rotunda bench and two broken vending machines. It was a wasteland.

"Now we know why it's called The Pits," Angie said. "No country songs about this old place." She tapped on a sun-damaged map of Florida that hung behind plexiglass. It looked decades old.

"Let's haul ass," Josiah said.

"No matter where we go, we're always running, we're always hauling ass," Angie said. She sighed, loud enough so he'd hear.

The utility room Nolan told them about was to the left of the women's restroom, behind an unlocked door and up two broken steps in front of floor-to-ceiling columns with peeling paint. The padlock wasn't worth shit on the old door. Inside, the room was rectangular with a flickering overhead light, about half the size of a standard garage, grey, concrete. The electric water pump hummed next to the generator, surrounded by propane and gallons of bleach. There was a ladder, several yard rakes and a broken mailbox. Bingo—their shovels and canvas gloves.

Angie was the first to scream when she saw it: a severed head lay by a row of shovels near the water pump. Josiah was so shocked that his mouth hung open. No sound came at all. Blood pooled around the human head, puddling into the wheels of a steel wire shelf, racked with power tools, boxes of toilet paper, and insect repellent. The eyeball in the head hung from a veined spongy nerve, dangling down by the chin. Its mouth was open, showing the teeth still intact, stained with blood. The other eye was open, staring lifelessly and colorlessly to nowhere.

Angie instinctively grabbed Josiah as they stumbled backward, eyes roving the utility room for s*omething*, someone. A human head . . .

"We gotta go!" Josiah cried, grabbing the shovels and canvas gloves.

They dumped the supplies into the Chevy. They locked the car doors.

"Nolan's not fucking around!" Angie said. "Did you see that?"

"Yeah, that's the kid—

"The kid that was killed. That radio girl just said they were looking for his head! We've gotta tell somebody."

Josiah reversed, hitting the gas. "Shut your mouth about all of it, Angie! We didn't see nothing! We're not telling nobody nothing! Our fingerprints are all over that room now! Did you forget we're wanted in Montgomery and Knoxville for stealing? Mountain View? Jesus Christ, Angie, you don't think!"

"His, his eye—"

They were back on Mowry, speeding down the moonlit road. "You didn't see nothing. Got it?"

Angie cried the whole way to Barrett's Cemetery. Josiah parked at the curb, his hands shaking. The two of them worked on autopilot, heaving the shovels and canvas gloves out of the backseat, quickly running toward the cemetery.

"Cop car. Get down, baby," Josiah said, pulling her down with him behind some palmettos. They hightailed it over a paddock fence and into the woods. The gutters were choked with leaves from yesterday's rain, and the cold air suddenly made Angie freeze. The air was smokey from the mill. She thought about dropping the shovel and running, running even from Josiah. This was too much. What had she gotten herself into?

"Wonder what this girl did to get murdered," Josiah said.

"You don't do nothing to get murdered," Angie said. "Are you crazy, talking like that?"

They came upon the rows of headstones. There was nobody around, just like Nolan had promised. It was easy finding the grave marked Margot "Babes" Henry, now almost a week old. The flashlight was their only source of light.

"There she is," Angie said. "The grave."

"One missing headstone ain't gonna make her less dead," Josiah said. "Keep a lookout while I dig."

"Don't you think that's sad? A boy and girl from the same

school?"

He huffed. "I don't got time right now to feel sad, Angie Johnson."

They moved like animals, fast in the dark.

III

When Jane found out about the fair, she completely lost her shit. She held a stony expression on the drive home, exploding the minute she and Letty walked through the door. It was now 2:00 a.m. She hustled around the kitchen holding a cup of decaf.

"Mom," Letty said. She slouched on the couch. "You're freaking out for no reason."

Jane was still in polyester pink, hair tied up with a ribbon. She grabbed a string of orange twinkle lights. "The sheriff called the diner at one in the morning to tell me my kid is in *custody* for being out past curfew."

"They said the curfew was lifted!"

"I had to leave my job early—the job that pays the rent for this dump—and pray to Jesus, Mary, and Joseph that Sugar Bends patrol doesn't fine *me* for my daughter's disregard to the law. I had to pick up my daughter from the police station at a time like this!"

"I know, Mom."

"And I recall forbidding you to be out after school hours until this murder madness was over. Did you forget? Why the hell did you lie?"

Letty sighed. "I know, Mom. But it was just me, Bernie, and Cam. We weren't doing anything wrong, for real. A few rides and we were gonna come right home. Cam even wore a watch so we could keep checking the time."

Jane laughed, plugging in the lights. The kitchen illuminated with a soft orange glow. "He wore a watch. How considerate."

"You're overreacting."

"I'm underreacting, Letty. I'm furious." Jane poured what was left of the decaf, dumping the carafe into the sink.

"It wasn't supposed to be a big deal. We didn't know about the bad stuff going on with Everett Myers until after we were already at the fair!"

"*Bad stuff going on,*" Jane said. She kicked off her shoes. "Food poisoning can get filed under 'bad stuff,' Letty. Losing a job, that's bad stuff. Our community and neighbors getting killed off one at a time, that's not bad stuff, it's irreversible!"

"I know, Mom."

"Another child was murdered, Letty! Do you not understand that?"

"I know," Letty said. "It was dumb."

"This is the dumbest thing you've ever done," Jane said. She let down her long red hair, pacing. "I wouldn't even send you to school if I didn't have to."

"I know."

"Here I am, on my lunch hour going to the drug store to pick up some festive lights to make your Halloween at home a little special—just a little bit. For four ninety-nine, that's hard to do."

"I know."

"And you're out with your friends in the middle of the night!"

"It wasn't even the middle of the night! That's not true!"

Jane sighed. It was almost 2:30 a.m., when everything felt shut off and quiet and dark. Lamplight filled the room. She joined Letty on the couch.

"I don't want to go to work, I don't want you attending school. I want to rent a moving van and get out of Sugar Bends where we'll be safe. But it's impossible."

"I know, Mom."

Jane turned toward her daughter, softening her voice. "No more sneaking off with your friends, no more bicycling to the cemetery. You go to school and you come home."

Letty lowered her gaze. "Fine."

"I brought home a pumpkin so we could make another jack-o-lantern," Jane said. It was round and barely scuffed below the stem. "You promise me you're not going out anymore. It's too dangerous. Men hide in the bushes; one strike with that hammer, you're out."

"I said '*I promise*,'" Letty whined.

Jane locked eyes with her daughter, engulfed with sadness. At times like these, she extra- missed Hank. She wanted to tell him about this argument—Letty's Famous Arrest, which wasn't even close to an arrest, but gosh, they'd be up all night talking about it if he were alive. And if she were being honest with herself, Hank would get a big laugh out of the whole thing.

"I'm not going, anyway—to the cemetery. Bernie, she's not so into Talking Dead Society anymore. She thinks it's dumb. We're getting too old for that stuff."

Jane softened her gaze then, too. "I'm sorry to hear that. Are you getting too old for that, too?"

"I guess so."

"Your dad would've been up in arms over this, Letty. Don't think he would've found this escapade of yours the least bit amusing."

"I know."

They hugged tightly, and Letty cried in her mother's arms about riding in the police car and how scared she was. "I can't hear him so much anymore."

"Who? Your father?"

"No matter how much I practice listening to him, or feeling him close, nothing comes."

Jane held her close, kissing her forehead and stroking her hair in soft strokes until she settled down. It was inconceivable to imagine anything happening to Letty. "He can hear you, honey."

IV

L etty decided not to tell her mom about Nolan Craven on the Ferris wheel. Not even about the black eyes. It seemed weird to bring it up at a time like this, and her mom had enough to think about. It would just tip her over the edge. She lay awake looking at the half-moon from her bed. The view used to be blocked by a mango tree that curled around the trellis. It was nothing more now than a short stump; a storm had cut the bark in half over the summer.

Nolan Craven hadn't been creepy, Letty decided. He was grieving, too, just like she was. It wasn't fair to think he was a creeper. And he only looked giant to her because they were up so high up on the Ferris wheel. The rides used to make her dizzy at the fair and now she was imagining things.

She pulled a lavender blanket up to her chin, trying not to cry again. What if the killer came after her mother when her mother was at work? What if he hid in the pantry or the kitchen, or underneath the car, like what happened in the first murder, Clint Ramirez, the guy who lived off Reed and Mowry? Where would she live if her mom was killed? Maybe her mom had money in a bank someplace so Letty could pay the rent if she died. Maybe that's how it worked. Her face hurt

147

from crying so much.

Letty thought about Babes Henry, wishing Babes would give her a sign in the form of a shooting star, or even a small voice inside her head, that everything would be okay. She and her mother would be okay, and the serial killer wouldn't get to them. This would end. Sugar Bends would go back to the way it was.

Letty wanted the sadness to be over.

Her mind drifted to other things. She tossed the blanket off when it got too warm. She imagined a boy beside her in bed. The thought was embarrassing, stupid, definitely gross. She laughed her ass off about it, stifling her giggles with a pillow smashed against her face. She playfully punched the pillow. Who would she date once high school came? Nobody, it was too stupid. Babes Henry dated Everett Myers and look what happened to her!

An hour after Letty fell asleep, she was woken by footsteps. She sat up in bed. She could tell by the sounds it wasn't her mother. Somebody else was in the house.

"Dad?" Maybe it was the promise Nolan Craven had made coming true. Maybe he was giving her a visit. It was about time.

"Dad, is that you?"

Letty opened her bedroom door. Orange, twinkling lights

cast shadows on the wooden floor. It was too dark to see. But she heard him.

Nolan Craven.

"Theo Shortridge. I've got you now."

Nolan lunged out of the darkness and into the shotgun hallway, the shiny hammer raised above his head.

IV

Theo awoke to the sound of the dead pumping in her ears like a hydraulic machine. She'd never experienced such turbulence in her skull. She cupped her hands over her ears, afraid she wouldn't be able to get rid of the noise. Somebody must have died on their street. Or somebody beyond the grave wanted her undivided attention. Nancy? She sprinted out of the house and into the yard. She sighed in relief at the sight of Jane and Letty standing by the mailbox surrounded by police, including Sheriff Baez. Sirens squawked and a few minutes later, Loxahatchee Road was crawling with emergency vehicles.

The Hillbilly Hammer.

"Nolan Craven," Theo said.

She'd observed during Babes Henry's cleanup that the investigations were getting shorter. They didn't even call in a detective from Tallahassee anymore, not since Trevor Winston's murder back at the start of summer. And the Hillbilly Hammer knew it. He knew how Sugar Bends was handling it. Poorly.

Hours later, at 5:00 a.m., Theo sat with Letty while Jane, in fresh hysteria, hammered plywood over the windows. She sat with her legs curled under her, Letty lying on the couch with her blanket, the TV turned to *I Love Lucy*. Lucy and Ethel were heaving a giant bass between hotel rooms, and the studio audience roared in laughter. Letty watched in silence.

"Mom's drill is on the fritz," Letty said. She set a half-empty glass of milk on the table.

Theo looked over her shoulder toward the kitchen window as the sirens and blue and red lights cut off. Two patrol cars were parked on Loxahatchee. They'd be there all day, probably through tomorrow.

"Letty, what happened?"

Letty's eyes met Theo's. "You know what happened. He almost got me. It happened so fast."

"Was it the same man you told me about the other night? At the gas station?"

Letty sniffled. "You gotta promise not to tell my mom. She's already flipped."

"Shoot."

"It was the same guy. But I saw him again. I went to the fair—me and my friends snuck out. He was on the Ferris wheel. He asked me for a favor, and I messed up real bad."

Theo's body tensed with fear. "What was the favor?"

"He said if I told him everything about you, he'd let me hear my dad's voice again. He kept saying he worked with my dad. I told him where you lived because he asked me. I was scared to say no. He thought this was *your* house," Letty said, shamefully.

"Your mom didn't raise an idiot, but you listen to me, kid. You need to leave this alone. You stay away from this."

"What do you mean?"

"Nolan Craven is the Hillbilly Hammer. But he's not like you and me. He's hypnotizing us somehow—making us see things that aren't there."

"Black confetti," Letty whispered.

"I saw Nancy like she was right in front of me, like I could reach out and touch her. He knows things about me he shouldn't. He's killing for something—and he wants to get close to me. Maybe to you, too, but I'm not going to let him." Theo looked over her shoulder, making sure Jane wasn't within earshot, even though the racket was enough to know she was outside.

Letty's eyes filled with tears. She wiped them away. Theo could tell Letty didn't want to cry in front of her.

"Why? Why's all this happening? How did he know my name? How did he know my *dad*?"

Theo raised an eyebrow. "I don't think he did. Maybe he

worked with your dad, sure, but I think he gets a reading on a person—energy waves or something, a kind of psychic ability— and he uses it against you. You leave all of this to me and keep your ass at home."

"But what about Nancy?"

"I don't know. Nancy's not dead. But he's got her; he's got her somewhere."

Letty frowned. "You can't hear her."

Theo shook her head.

When Letty fell asleep, Theo joined Jane. She tried not to grimace at the hammer that Jane clutched in her hand, bashing the plywood. If Letty hadn't run when she did . . . maybe loving other people wasn't worth it, Theo thought. Maybe the toll on your soul was too much. She grabbed a second hammer and helped Jane cover the rest of her house. They didn't get done until three hours later, when it was time for each of them to go to work.

OCTOBER 29

I

The morning after the fair, Everett Myers's murder was announced to a sleeping Sugar Bends. Most people would awake to Tricia Cross announcing the death on the radio, the rest of their day shaken by the Hillbilly Hammer. Sawyer, however, already knew. He had awoken in the middle of the night to one missed call and texts from each of the Scarecrows. Tricia had been the only one not to text or call, maybe because it was the middle of the night and she was working at the station, but when he'd sensed her absence, he got dressed and drove to the lighthouse at half past four to see for himself she was okay.

The murder had happened under their noses, literally. His blood ran cold.

And once again, Sugar Bends is grieving. I'm Tricia Cross and you're listening to 101.1. Let's take it slow today. We're in a dark time. Take care of each other.

Tricia hit the control panel and removed her headphones. Sawyer had made coffee, and the room filled with its warm and robust scent. The morning light seeped through the bay windows, shining on the freshwater marshes bordering Lake Briggs. The sky was the color of grapefruit. Tricia and Sawyer kissed, Sawyer smoothing her hair back.

"He decapitated him," Tricia said softly, intertwining her fingers with Sawyer's.

"Good morning to you, too."

"Don't joke right now." Tricia pulled away from his embrace, gazing out the window at the town, a lane of traffic appearing ant-size from their viewpoint on Griffin.

Sawyer watched her watching the town, and it dawned on him it hadn't been until that middle-of-the-night text from Ben Ashcroft—*another murder*—how afraid he was of scaring Tricia off. It wasn't just her husband, Fischer. Fischer was in the picture, but he wasn't Tricia's whole picture. Her idea of a perfect and fulfilling relationship was the one they had now, hiding from the rest of the world, being cooped up in a lighthouse come nighttime. It wasn't sustainable. It wasn't even healthy. Whatever she was willing to give him, he'd take it in earnest.

"Town's going to be at war," Sawyer said. He poured coffee for each of them; they both took it black. "I've got to be at the school in two hours and it's the last place I want to be right now."

"Can we leave?" Tricia said, dreamily. She laughed at herself, and Sawyer knew she was only half-kidding. "A serial killer isn't going to follow two forty-somethings that don't know what the hell they're doing with their life."

"I'm thirty-nine," Sawyer said.

"Mister's ready for retirement." She smiled.

"The Hillbilly Hammer wouldn't follow us, but our problems would follow us." He handed Tricia her coffee mug. "I've got an inkling about this Hillbilly Hammer guy. When you were on the air, it got me thinking."

"Sounds like Scarecrows are due for a meeting."

"No, this can't wait. I've got to tell somebody and you're the only one I trust."

Tricia sipped from the mug. "Is this about that man you saw in the hedges?"

"Come with me."

Sawyer didn't tell Tricia where they were headed. When they arrived at the sugarcane mill, he parked in the pumpkin patch across the road. Wagons were loaded up with pumpkins and witches made of fabric. A ghost made of mesh blew in the wind, attached to a broken signpost: PUMPKINS SOLD HERE.

"The mill?" Tricia asked.

They crossed the road, climbing over the guardrail. The machine noise from the tractors and lifts was silenced by an alarm going off at the mill: shift change. The tractor engines rumbled between the stalks, and the acrid stench of smoke and fire was in the air. Sawyer took Tricia's hand, and they walked quickly through the sugarcane stalks. Leaves stuffed in the pockets of the stalks scratched their legs as they walked through the dirt.

"There's another burn the day after tomorrow. The harvest begins soon after that," Sawyer said. They came to a partial clearing, out of breath. "Burning season goes until March."

"Yeah, the black rain. What's your point?" A lick of sweat beaded Tricia's forehead.

"A guy named Nolan Craven died here during the controlled burnings in 1988. He worked at the mill, lived in town. He was buried at Barrett's. And I don't know how, but I think he's back. Maybe he was never really buried. You know how the dark side gets to Sugar Bends, Trish, it's not crazy."

"I'm with you. Keep going."

Sawyer wiped his forehead with the back of his arm, sighing. "The Hillbilly Hammer is more than just a psychopath blending into the town."

"He's rising from the dead."

"No, I don't think he ever really died. He wants something from somebody here. It runs deeper than just killing. I'm not convinced Nancy Russo's dead or left the state, or whatever they want to say. There's more at work here."

"You feel it," Tricia said.

"When I saw that man in the rawhide jacket, he didn't look like he was from this time. I can't explain it. But there was electricity coming from him, an insatiable energy. I should've followed him when I had the chance."

"I believe you."

"Seven deaths and one missing person in ten months— gotta be a record," Sawyer said. "He wants something, but what?"

"I've got one question for you, Sawyer. Why the hell did he decapitate that boy? Wasn't it enough to just kill him?"

Sawyer and Tricia embraced; fingers intertwined. They were already sticky from the heat. "Time to batten down the hatches and find that bastard," Sawyer said.

II

Josiah managed to heave the headstone, dripping with wet leaves, and smudged in soil, into the motel room. Nobody saw him or Angie. It had been too awkward and heavy to lift into the bathtub as planned, so they dragged it past the double bed and against the wall. When Angie tried mentioning the bloodied head from the utility room in conversation, Josiah turned the TV up full blast: one of those feel-good family shows from thirty years ago that played nonstop, even at 7:00 a.m.

"You still mad at me?" Josiah said. He'd been too nervous to sit down with Angie on the bed.

"Yeah, Joey, I'm mad at you. You don't even care about that girl that died. You don't care that we saw some guy's head cut off. They were people once!"

"Lots of people die every day. Why you got such a boner for death all of a sudden?"

"Don't say that."

Josiah clicked his tongue. He peered through the blinds for the hundredth time, waiting for Nolan to get his ass over here, collect this headstone, and give them their money. They'd be out of here in a matter of hours, tops. He never wanted to see this town again.

"What would you do if I died?" Angie asked. She curled her hair around her index finger. "Like if I got murdered like that girl. Would you be sad?"

"Yeah, I'd be sad. Cut it out."

"I'm sick of this. Tired of trouble." She rolled her eyes.

Josiah snorted. "That so? Well, you decide what the hell you're gonna do. I'm going for a walk. I don't need this."

He walked out the door, hands stuffed in his pockets. The tallgrass prairie across the road was coated in shades of orange. The Mayday Motel sign flickered in the dusty daylight. He thought about his mama back home. "My pressure's up," she used to say, while all the kids on the street tugged at her house dress, asking for cookies or eggs, or Band-Aids, or a drink. He wondered if his pressure was going up with all this, if that was even really a thing, or just something mothers said.

He pulled his hat tightly down over his forehead, wisps of blond hair sticking out the sides. He got to the dump, wishing he had a cigarette to light up for himself.

"Good morning," Nolan said, flicking a lighter's spark wheel under Josiah's mouth. A cigarette suddenly appeared between his lips.

Josiah gasped, and the cigarette nearly fell off his lip. "Shit, you scared the daylights out of me."

Nolan tucked the lighter in his fringy pocket. Josiah noticed, up close, he smelled like firewood.

"About that rest stop place you sent us to—"

"I could feel the headstone hitch when you pulled it out of the earth," Nolan said. "Thank you for doing me the favor."

The heat was searing, even in the shade.

"You got my money?"

"Check your pockets."

Josiah exhaled, flicking the ash. He didn't appreciate the funny games, but he wasn't about to question it to a man capable of decapitating somebody. Sure enough, two wads of cash bundled in parchment were stuffed inside his pockets.

Nolan gazed off into the prairie. "I'm ready to tell you what I want."

Josiah fingered through the cash, short of breath as he nervously stuffed it into his jeans. Now they could scram. "Yeah, what now?"

"I'm looking for an apprentice. Somebody to aid me in storing others' grief inside themselves. Somebody to breathe that grief into me in exchange for immortality, freedom from feeling any amount of grief themselves, or feeling anything other than the utmost comforts. I need more of it. That's why

I've returned to Sugar Bends."

A whiff of burning earth billowed up from the ground. Josiah coughed uncontrollably. On the final heave, as his chest swelled with blazing heat he dropped the cigarette, and its flame went out. Before his eyes, Nolan Craven transitioned into an old man, his skin charred purple and black like a fresh bruise, his face sunken from severe burns. The October air was like grasping oven coils with your bare hands. Nolan's stone eyes flickering black. He was decaying.

Josiah nearly choked on his own tongue, but in a blink, Nolan returned to his pseudo-normal self. He straightened his eyeglasses and looked down at Josiah, who was kneeling in the dirt.

"How would you like to come work with me?"

III

A ngie had gone looking for Josiah when he hadn't returned right away. When she saw Nolan with Josiah gallivanting by the dumpster, she turned back, and got dressed, grabbed the gun. She palmed its grip and thumbed back the hammer. Her heart pounded.

"Hi, mister," Angie trembled, as the two men walked through the motel room door. The TV was still on. She resisted the urge to make a run for it. "The headstone is right over there, by the bed."

Nolan nodded. "You worked remarkably hard."

"Thank you," Angie said, wanting to be polite. She looked at Josiah. He was winter pale. "Joey?" she whispered. "What's the matter with you?"

Nolan wiped his lenses with the hem of his jacket. He put canvas gloves on and reached for Babes Henry's headstone with Christmas-morning delight.

"You're scaring me. Say something, why don't you." Angie put the handgun in the waistband of her paisley skirt, doing the exact opposite of what her cousin Billy taught her about firearm safety. She couldn't be in this room with this killer another minute. She took Josiah by the wrist and led him out the motel room door.

He staggered a foot behind her as they headed to the Chevy. Angie retrieved the keys from Josiah's pocket, shakily unlocking the door.

"Joey, what did he say to you? Say something. You got the money?"

Josiah flopped into the passenger side and Angie leaned over to click his seatbelt in place. The money stuck out of his jeans carelessly, like grocery coupons or movie tickets. She grabbed the cash out of his jeans, stuffing it into the glove compartment—two equal stacks, fifty thousand dollars.

"Bye, Mayday Motel," she said, hitting the gas, heading toward the exit ramp on Sidewinder to I-75.

The silence between them was broken by an engine rumbling in the distance. Angie grimaced, smacked with fear. She'd know that sound anywhere. Her father, the Ramblin' Man, was cruising down the highway.

"No," she cried. "No, no, no—it can't be."

She made the turnoff onto Sidewinder, hitting the gas until the needle went to ninety miles per hour. "Joey, it's Mitch!"

The handgun wouldn't be much help from the driver's seat, especially if she didn't want to spend a lifetime in jail. She was no sharpshooter. Angie honked the horn, her face sunburn-red as she screamed at Josiah.

"Wake up!" she said.

Ramblin' Man inched closer. Gravel dust filled the air around the Chevy. She could taste it. She looked over her shoulder, and the Ramblin' Man wasn't there. She could hear his old hog, the sound inexplicably guttural, so close like she was on the bike herself. That same sound she'd known since childhood. All of Morristown knew the sound of that bike. The noise rattled the roof of the car. The metallic flapping made it sound like it was gonna pop off. Ramblin' Man got closer. But where? That horrible, guttural sound.

And then in a flash, Angie looked over her shoulder and it wasn't the same bike she knew from back home in Tennessee. It looked military, something out of *Mad Max: Fury Road*, a war machine. She looked in the rear view, and the vehicle vanished as swiftly as it had appeared, that husky engine roaring in the background.

"Please, stop," Angie cried. *Nolan*. Had to be. It was. She merged lanes, dodging an eighteen-wheeler. The driver blared the horn aggressively. She jerked the truck back onto the road. Her curls blew in the wind, but Josiah looked out the window with chilling indifference. He'd turned white, unfocused like he was sedated, like the last thing on earth he cared about was getting out of here alive. Angie called his name, but he didn't hear her. His palms were open in his lap as if surrendering.

IV

Angie and Josiah sat in hardback chairs in the booking office at the Sugar Bends police department, listening to the sheriff and deputy outside the room. Angie was arrested on reckless driving. When the squad arrived at the scene on Sidewinder, they thought Josiah was hammered because he was unresponsive, barely replying to their questions. His breathalyzer was clean, and an EMT declared him healthy.

"You think they're suspects?" said Deputy Dawn Saxson. Half-grinning, she plopped a file onto the reception desk. "Please tell me you don't. I know you want to catch this killer, but let's get real."

Fischer chuckled. "Nah, not these kids."

He sipped from a mug of microwaved, day-old coffee. He waltzed into the booking office to talk to the two detainees.

"So, we've got no identification, no driver's license, and your registration expired three weeks ago. What were you doing out riding like maniacs anyway?"

Angie's lip trembled. She shut her eyes tightly and sniffled, composing herself. "I wasn't paying no attention," she said.

"At least you're honest," Fischer said, scribbling notes.

"Makes my job easier. Your handgun was confiscated. It's unregistered. Big shocker."

"Did the Chevy get towed?" Angie asked. "Where is it?"

Fischer didn't look up from his paperwork. He took a swig of coffee. "You mean the motorcycle?"

"Motorcycle?" Angie said. "We don't got a motorcycle. There was a motorcycle chasing us."

Fischer raised an eyebrow, pushing a file between them. "You were arrested doing 90 on a Triumph Bonneville with the inscription *Ramblin' Man* on the side. Does that jog your memory?"

V

Theo blasted Black Flag, "Black Coffee." She needed the song like she needed an IV of black coffee and a hot shower. She'd spent the morning planting safety defenses for herself if the Hillbilly Hammer returned. She wasn't a gun owner—Nancy would've justifiably given her grief about it, considering how much gun-related carnage she'd scrubbed over the years—so she slipped a chef's knife under her mattress, closest to where her head rested. She stashed a baseball bat with Jose Canseco's autograph on it in the living room. The year 1988 was good for him; maybe that luck would rub off on Theo. She walked around the house touching Nancy's possessions. She smelled Nancy's clothes, even what of hers was in the hamper, unwashed since December. She smelled her shampoo bottles, cradled in the same corner of the shower. Shea butter and passion fruit. She opened jewelry boxes and went through drawers, and even puttered around on Nancy's laptop, like a big secret might expose what really happened to her the morning she disappeared.

Theo touched a miniature hand-carved wooden rocking horse, bathed in sunlight, that had been sitting in the windowsill for two decades. She couldn't remember who gave it to Nancy.

Maybe it was something she bought at the farmer's market, or a garage sale. The craftsmanship on the little thing was remarkable; thick yarn for the mane and leather saddle sewn into the base. Theo missed Nancy so much: their private laughter, their gags, their romance, their infinite love.

A missed call from Roberta called Theo out of her reverie. She hit the redial button. "It's me."

"Took you long enough, chief. We need you now: you know why."

A half hour later, Theo locked up and hopped in the van, turning off Loxahatchee Road. A news reporter from Hounds was interviewing the sheriff—that scuzzy Fischer Baez—about the decapitation. She flipped off the radio and her Bluetooth kicked in. Nothing quite scared her like the real-life nightmares around town.

When she arrived at the woods near the Tidioute trailer park, the bass gave a static snap when she cut the engine. The cool evening of yesterday had risen to a stuffy eighty-two degrees, and the smell of impending rain was in the air.

"Welcome aboard," Roberta said. They hugged for the first time since December. In Ben Ashcroft's trailer, the world felt awfully grim.

Theo had history with the Scarecrows: Ben Ashcroft, Roberta Quentin, Tricia Cross, and Sawyer Harris. Felt like she knew them longer than her own parents. True, she blamed them for not carrying out Nancy's search party with more aggression. They could keep watch over Sugar Bends and all its insurmountable dark corners, but they couldn't locate her beautiful wife after she was snatched by a killer in front of the citrus and nursery.

"Smells like soup's on," Theo said. The music was off, but her ears still rang.

There were cabbages, radishes, carrots, and apples in bunches next to a whistling coffee maker.

"Rabbit's soup," Roberta said. "Okay for summer, tastier after the cane harvest. Welcome back."

"That's called carpenter's soup," Tricia said. "All's missing is poblanos."

Theo's body felt stiff and disjointed. She didn't want to sit down, not now. The trailer wasn't spacious, but it was cozy and always had a residual toasty smell of coffee and cigarettes. Everything in the house was old, even the dog. Ben and Sawyer sat on a plaid couch. Roberta leaned against the front door; Tricia stood by a kitchen countertop refilling coffee.

They took turns hugging Theo for a long time, longer than

she felt comfortable with, given how incensed she'd been at them in the last year. But it was the warmth from another human's touch that edged on rejuvenation.

When nobody loved you, human touch was a rare oasis.

Roberta Quentin was the youngest Scarecrow, and the newest member. She was a full- time homemaker and part-time waitress at Hunky Dory's. Her kids were the splendor of her life: Sarah, nine, Abigail, seven, and Walker, five. Her bartender husband, Steve, moved to Detroit a couple years ago, and she'd been on her own ever since, although they'd never formally divorced. Roberta considered herself everybody's second mom in Sugar Bends, carpooling kids all over the place, to sports and school and barbecues.

Roberta was introduced to Sugar Bends's gray area during a Fourth of July parade on Placerville back in 2011. Her sister, Rena Buckner, disappeared. Rena and Steve had been standing on the sidewalk waving frilly American flags, watching the homemade parade floats drive by. Roberta, to this day, said she'd blinked, and Rena was gone, like a light switch. Steve, on the other hand, refused to talk about it after the investigation, which closed even faster than Nancy's.

"Let's not beat around the bush," Theo said. "Being here sucks for me. You shits betrayed me and let Nancy down. But

I want this motherfucker stopped."

Ben nodded. "Glad to have you back."

Tricia lifted her coffee mug in salute.

Theo felt a pang of guilt for her exasperation, but she'd never show it. They didn't seem surprised. Guess they knew her better than she thought.

Ben said, "Roberta and I have brainstormed the Hillbilly Hammer's victims' whereabouts—and the lack of evidence."

"Spoiler alert: we came up short," Roberta smirked.

"My guess is that he's an organized killer that's aware of police procedural—almost militant about it," Ben said. "Most serial murderers are not impulsive, and this man is no exception. There's no tracing him. The last killer in this town was Jonah Truman, in 1993. After he retired from the Sugar Bends police academy, he moved to Hounds, but came back here to knock a few off. Why did he do that? Because he knew the town like the back of his hand. But even with his expert knowledge, he got caught. He made mistakes."

"That's where the metaphysical comes in," Roberta said.

"Metaphysical?" Theo said. "Not in Sugar Bends."

Roberta raised her coffee mug in unity, continuing. "This killer's triggered by something—or someone—here. Maybe it's psychic abilities, albeit as seldom as they are at times."

"Lots of people are psychic. They just don't know it, or they don't practice," Theo said.

Roberta shook her head. "I don't think that's it. I think he's trying to see which murder will illicit the most grief, the most sorrow. He got to Babes Henry, then murdered again two weeks later. Another teenager."

"Maybe the grief gives him power to disappear without a trace," Tricia suggested.

"It's possible," Ben said.

Roberta picked up and shook Hijinx's bowl, the pup circling around her legs before stuffing his nose in the dish. "We talked about when Clint Ramirez died, and Christy Lyons. They had nothing in common except they both drove by the mill and lumber yard to get to work. Clint Ramirez worked at the post office, and Christy Lyons was a massage therapist in Hounds."

Theo shrugged. "What about the old woman? Phyllis Kratt?"

"Phyllis Kratt had barely left her house in the last year. She was on dialysis and broke her hip. She got her groceries and prescriptions delivered. Seems random," Roberta said.

"One thing is certain, each of us has come in contact with this man before," Sawyer said.

"Nolan Craven," Theo said. "That's his name, Nolan

Craven."

"You know him, too," Tricia said.

"I might have—" Theo sighed. "—met him at his house on Cinder. He called me about a cleanup job; his mother was murdered."

"Was his mother Phyllis Kratt?" Ben asked.

"No, this was a new death; blood spores were present," Theo said.

Theo skipped over the part about Nancy coming back to life. That was hers. And if Nolan Craven was capable of black magic, he had a spiritual side that was stronger than she could ever dream of honing. Cooperating with him would be worth it, to her. She had nothing to lose and didn't want to hear it from the Scarecrows. Everything haunted that happened between her and Nolan, she'd keep it that way: a secret. Just in case. Just in case he could really make Nancy come back.

"Rawhide jacket," Sawyer said.

"Mustache like this—" Tricia hand-mimed, her eyes turning cold.

"Has a coyote," Roberta said.

"Has a coyote or manifests himself into a coyote?" Ben said.

"I think he has a coyote," Roberta said. "I saw one staring into my mud room the other night. I was folding laundry. The kids fell asleep watching *The Wizard of Oz*. I got one look at that coyote and its eyes were—"

"Black," Tricia said.

Roberta nodded. "Black, predatory, wrath. And it was wrath for me. It seemed personal."

"He's spying on you," Ben said. "Maybe he enjoys that part of it. Maybe it gets his rocks off, the son of a gun."

"Jesus Christ," Tricia said.

Roberta, like Theo, had experienced her share of bizarre happenings. She'd witnessed the infamous Sugar Bends snowstorm in 1981, and the hailstorm in 1996 during peak hurricane August.

"What about Babes Henry and Everett Myers?" Theo said. "Both teenagers, both attended the same school, might have dated once or twice."

"I don't see any connections besides those," Ben said. "And thanks to Sawyer's detective work, although they were in the same graduating class, we know they didn't share any of the same classes or electives. Everett Myers wasn't attending school much."

Sawyer sighed, leaning backward on the sofa. He told the story of Nolan Craven and the cane field burning at the mill in 1988. The ghost's appearance was a way to maintain the illusion he was still a living, twenty-something-year-old man. The fire and the burns had sparked a malevolency within his antisocial personality. What he'd come back for, or how long he'd watched them, was uncertain.

"What do we do?" Tricia said. "Just keeping watch isn't doing anybody any favors."

Ben said, "We pay attention. We go into town; we watch as rigidly as he's watched us. He's out there. Maybe he's at the mill. This afternoon, I'm headed to the mill to see if I can get a roster of everybody that currently works there. Maybe Hans and Bethany will let me look at some night security footage."

"Dream on," Roberta said, laughing.

"Theo," Sawyer said, in a low voice. "When you went to Nolan Craven's house for that cleanup, what was the address?"

"Cinder Street. Wedged between two other houses." Theo pulled out her phone, thumbing around for the address. "He lived at 786 Cinder Street."

Sawyer exchanged glances with Tricia. "At 786? That can't be. There's only two cracker houses and the apartment complex on Cinder, and the addresses start with two. One of my colleagues lives there."

"He's right. I used to live on Cinder. Two houses," Ben said, and Roberta agreed on the location.

"So, what, you think he sent me to a house that wasn't his? That doesn't make sense," Theo said.

"I think it's his tricks. His hypnotism, whatever it is that he's absorbed from, gives him the capability. Hey, quiet," Ben hushed.

Suddenly, there was a clattering on the roof. Footfalls on the asphalt shingles. Ben put a finger to his pursed lips, signifying silence. Theo crossed her arms, her body filling with terror.

"He's listening. He's here. He's on the roof," Sawyer whispered.

Nolan's heavy footsteps were interrupted by several minutes of silence. The Scarecrows heard only the rustling of the twisted laurel oak branches against the singles. Then, the footfalls started again, longer strides. Theo side-eyed the window by the plaid couch, waiting for him to burst through with the raised hammer and mad eyes.

Five minutes went by. The Scarecrows waited and listened. Nolan's footfalls grew quieter, then stopped altogether. Sawyer gestured to the window by the plaid couch where the six of them congregated, knees together, hands gripping lukewarm mugs and knees. Nolan sat on the roof above them, legs dangling over the edge. All they could see were his blue jeans and Chippewa boots.

"What the hell's he doing?" Tricia whispered.

"He's trying to scare us," Ben said. "He's a careless old fool. Don't open that door, Roberta—you open it, a coyote will emerge from the bushes and bite the bridge of your nose off."

Nolan got up from time to time. He walked across the asphalt shingles. He'd sit back down with his legs dangling over the side. He cracked open a can of something. The wind picked up. Then, he vanished soundlessly, just as he'd arrived.

The Scarecrows agreed to meet back up in two days. They sensed a siege was coming. Doors locked. Bureaus and chairs were stuffed underneath bolted doors. With a bowl of rabbit's soup in the front seat with her, Theo blasted "Son of a Preacher Man" by Dusty Springfield, needing to see this house on Cinder Street for herself; needing any sound, any voice, any feeling other than the horror she felt deep within herself.

The apartment complex, Cinder Bends Apartments, was silent as a grave out front. Two houses, not four, like the Scarecrows said.

"No," Theo said. "It can't be. It's impossible."

Nolan's house and all evidence of him was gone, as if the house had never existed at all.

VI

The auditorium at Earl Jones Middle School was crammed with kids dressed in Halloween costumes, much to the dismay of half the faculty and parents. Putting the proverbial foot down was hardly the battle now, as rumors flew that Sugar Bends's town hall was announcing a mandatory lockdown at 11:00 a.m.

"Letty, you okay?" Cameron said. They'd heard about Letty's attack as soon as they got to school.

"I'm fine," Letty said.

But she was shaken to her core in a way she'd never felt before. She knew girls and women were attacked by angry men all the time. She was no different. Now she and Babes Henry shared something in common. Her mom wanted her to stay home from school, but Letty insisted on going because it was dress-up day. She was excited about her costume. Most of the kids didn't know who David Bowie was, and truth is, *she* barely knew either. She wore an orange geometric jumpsuit and red wig. She didn't own any boots, and certainly not platforms, so she wore her sixth-grade pair of red Converse sneakers that were a size too small. The best part was the red and blue lightning insignia lipsticked onto her forehead and cheekbone.

"Hike it up, Mr. Wheeler. Somebody's going to trip and

fall," Miss Carrigan said, as she directed the seventh graders into an empty row.

Cameron hitched up his Dickies, pulling the black polyester robe along with them. He hadn't taken off the white, gaping-mouthed ghost mask from *Scream* since homeroom.

"Bet your mom flipped her lid," Bernie said.

"Yeah."

"Mine grounded me for a month," Bernie sighed.

She promised she'd go as Shuri, the Black Panther, but her broken arm cast couldn't fit underneath the elastic of the black jumpsuit, so she cut the left arm's sleeves from elbow to wrist. On her right arm, she wore a gold wristband. The costume was complete with a holster and combat boots she'd taken from Joe without his permission.

"Next year, we ditch the fair and have our own fun," Cameron said.

"Yeah, we'll have to, 'cuz I can't believe the school hasn't thrown a shit fit over your costume," Bernie said.

Letty was between Cameron and Bernie. Principal Barlow asked students to quiet down, the sheriff would speak soon. "This is the least of their problems," Cameron said. "They're gonna announce early dismissal and cancel Halloween."

"Nuh-uh," Bernie said. "They can't do that. It's a national

holiday."

"Give me a break," Cameron said.

"You guys," Letty said. "Everett Myers died. The Hillbilly Hammer's out there—he came right for me. There are bigger problems here than candy."

Bernie scoffed. "I'm just glad it was a dickhole that got hammered this time. Everett Myers was everybody's nightmare. He was literally a nightmare in my nightmare."

"He owed me like sixteen bucks," Cameron agreed.

"Yeah, Letty, if it had to be somebody, may as well have been him," Bernie said, scratching into the crevice of her arm cast.

Principal Barlow and Sheriff Baez stood at the podium, with Miss Carrigan and Sawyer Harris hovering tensely at the corner of the stage.

"Good morning, students and staff, Sheriff Baez and Deputy Gonzalez. It is with a heavy heart I announce that our little town has lost another young soul: Everett Myers. Everett was one of our seniors. He died on October 27. I'm grieving, along with our faculty and the student body."

"Hear that?" Cameron whispered, looking over his shoulder. "It's the sound of Brick the Dick's absence. Who knows how long he's gonna be out for, with a murdered brother."

"Yeah, he's in mourning," Bernie laughed.

"Come on, guys, shut up," Letty said.

Miss Carrigan shot a curt look in their direction.

Principal Barlow cleared his throat. His face was red. He looked exhausted. "This is a tremendous loss for Sugar Bends, and for our students. Let's have a moment of silence for Everett Wayne Myers."

A few lone chuckles emerged from the eighth-grade row.

"Under normal circumstances, I'd tell you we have an early dismissal, and classes will resume tomorrow after a brief assembly with a grief counselor. However, this leads me into the next announcement, which I'm handing over to Sheriff Fischer Baez. I expect each of you to

give Sheriff Baez your undivided attention."

Letty surreptitiously peered down the row at the other seventh-grade class. Brick the Dick's absence was strange. It seemed wrong that something like that could happen to kids their age, but his brother was six years older. Everett Myers was dead. It didn't seem possible, and hearing it announced this way made it all the more real.

Sheriff Baez thanked Principal Barlow. "Without further ado, Sugar Bends will close at two o'clock this afternoon—

hold your crying for later—and school will be dismissed today as a stay-at-home order is put into effect through the rest of the week. Classes will resume Monday morning."

Bernie jumped out of her seat, pumping her good arm with the gold wristband. Her black curls bounced. "Holy shit, mandatory no school!"

Miss Carrigan shot another look. "Miss Acosta, sit down immediately!"

"Now, let's define what a stay-at-home order means for Sugar Bends. It doesn't mean hanging out with your friends or playing at the swimming pool or lake, or anywhere else. Everything, including the park and lake, will be closed until Monday. I'm talking businesses, recreation, sports, all frolicking. Halloween is cancelled. Gatherings and celebrations won't be tolerated. These orders will echo the stay-at-home orders we implemented during 2020 and the 2021 school year."

The auditorium went bonkers. Letty put her fingers in her ears.

"Bullshit!" Cameron cried.

"They can't do this!" said Bernie.

Miss Carrigan stepped up to the podium, shoving Sheriff Baez aside. "Quiet down, students. Or you'll be in detention until two."

"Curfew allowed us to implement safety protocols," Sheriff Baez continued. "But that's over. Now, it's mandatory. Shelter in place means you shelter for the next four days. If there's an emergency, you dial 911. We're doing this to better isolate the individual. We need your cooperation."

"Shit, this blows," Bernie said. She kicked the back of the seat in front of her.

"What about our candy exchange? What about our graveyard party?" Cameron said.

Sheriff Baez continued. "If an incident arises, we hope to catch the perpetrator. If you see anything suspicious, you can give us a call and somebody from the station will speak to you. Again, everything will close at two o'clock this afternoon. This means school is out once this assembly is over. You're going to go home in groups of no less than three. If you do not have anybody to walk with, you can come up to the stage and we'll arrange something."

Letty watched Mr. Harris in the wings of the stage. He looked glum. Surely, he knew something about Nolan Craven. She felt guilty for feeling sad about Halloween; it was just a kid's holiday, after all. It was one of those things, like summer, she'd always depended on. The stay- at-home order better work, she thought.

Cameron and Bernie started talking about ways they could still hang out on Halloween. Letty tried not to cry. She didn't want her David Bowie makeup to run.

Black Rain Season - Kayli Scholz

190

VII

The heat wave was sweltering. Theo hadn't remembered it being this hot last year, even days after a Category Two hurricane ripped up part of the Louisiana coast and made its way southeast. She'd driven straight from Cinder Street to The Pits, right next to the turnoff to Sidewinder. Fuck the lockdown, she thought. She was going to find out if Nolan Craven was full of shit or could bring Nancy back to life for her. The lockdown would take effect only a half hour from now.

Once Theo pulled into The Pits, there wasn't so much as a faraway car engine or humming tractor in the distance. Her sixth sense ticked into high gear at the entrance to the rest stop. Crabgrass was stinking in the sun. She cupped her hand over her right ear like a shell to crush the noise.

"Nolan?" Theo called. "If you've got Nancy, I want to see her before I enter this place."

The buzzing rhythmically increased when she pulled her hand away from her head. Her perception grayed, and she felt her spine and neck tingle with a breeze that wasn't there. Somebody had died here. But it sure as hell wasn't Nancy. She hadn't heard Nancy once in all this time.

Theo walked up the concrete pathway. Exploded boxes of smoked-out fireworks were all over the rotunda. She could smell the lumberyard from here, and the smoke from the fields a few miles away. She'd kept her promise: she hadn't gotten anybody involved and didn't have so much as a key on her body. She'd left the work van running. She had to know. She couldn't wait anymore for Nancy, for Nolan to give her Nancy. If Nancy wasn't here, if she wasn't in this decrepit rest stop, she'd drive to the sheriff station and give a report on Nolan Craven.

"Nancy?" Theo said.

The only vibration was an annihilating roar of static coming from behind the door marked ELECTRIC. She tried the door and, unsurprisingly, it was locked.

"Nancy? Nolan?"

Theo knew she'd been operating in a stupor of grief. People didn't come back from the dead, nor did they typically show up almost a year later, unharmed and as wonderful and tender as they'd ever been. She was desperate. Love had to bring Nancy back.

Theo stuck her head in the men's restroom. "Anybody here?" She went into the women's room. "Hello?"

The bathroom was stuffier inside than it was outside in the

flaming sunlight. At least out there, you'd catch a breeze every now and again. The twelve stalls were ceiling-high, directly across from twelve white sinks and motion-activated hand dryers. The brown paper towel dispenser was empty. There was a square window near the sinks, about twelve feet up from the ground.

Theo went into the middle stall and took a piss. When she was done, the faux steel lock wouldn't unlatch from the partition. It was stuck. She studied the grip, and it looked molded into the honeycomb-colored plastic partition. She fussed with the lock, pulling it forward and out of its latch. It didn't budge.

"Shit," Theo said.

She pushed into the door and the lock still didn't budge. She slammed her body weight into the door, and the partition walls shook, but the door remained closed. The trembling gave her a spec of hope the lock would give, so she slammed her shoulder into it again. Finally, she smacked the door with her fist. She was stuck in this restroom.

Theo sighed. She'd crawl out.

She got down on the grimy linoleum, the smell of filth under her nose. She went belly- first, attempting to stuff her head through the crawlspace. But there wasn't enough room to fit. She tried the other direction. She got on her back, hands to the floor, and slid feet-first, gliding forward. She only got as far as her shins and knees. She couldn't force it. There wasn't enough space.

"Goddamn it!"

Theo got off the floor. She estimated the stall was about three by four. Climbing was out of the question: it was too high, twelve feet off the ground. She stood on the toilet, figuring how much climbing or stretching was realistic to haul her body weight over the edge. She jumped, just to see what her hands could grasp, and nearly stumbled off the toilet seat. It was an impossible feat. There was no ledge to balance and climb on, either.

Theo felt in her pockets for her phone, which naturally, she'd left in the van, along with everything else.

"Hello?" she tried. "Anybody there?"

She kicked the latch in her steel-toed boots until the bridge of her foot hurt from the impact. Breathlessly, and now perspiring in the heat, she dropped to the floor to take a break.

VIII

hree hours crept by.

The heat was unremitting, an oven. Every few minutes, Theo would instinctively hitch her chin and inhale to take in "better air." She felt a modicum of relief doing so, imagining it was cooling her neck and arms. Sometimes, she'd hear an eighteen-wheeler ramble by, and she'd shout for help. A lot of good it did. She pounded her fist into the partition, but the lock barely rattled.

Theo could smell the problem. There was caulk sealing the lock and partition together. It was fresh, its scent as irritating and potent as bleach. She'd had her hands in enough cleanup jobs covering up crossfire shootings with caulk and related chemicals to know the difference: gunshots destroyed drywall and steel, a plastic partition would be easy to mess with. What she couldn't figure out was how she'd opened the door in the first place, and why the hell—or who the hell—had caulked it? Of course, she could guess. But she was too hot and sweaty to dwell on it. She just needed some relief.

"Sugar Bends, up to your old ways," Theo said. She knew her energy was better saved than spent pounding on the door, and kicking and shouting for men in trucks that couldn't hear her. God, it was hot. Her mouth was dry.

She shouldn't have come. She should've at least told the Scarecrows where she was going.

It was still daylight, late afternoon. Sunbeams splayed on the ceiling, penetrating the small round window in the ceiling corner. The lockdown was in full effect.

"You couldn't just piss yourself," Theo said, amused by the sound of her own voice.

Theo was thirsty, and she didn't want to think about how thirsty she was. Almost thirsty enough to consider drinking the toilet water. Almost. She'd never been so thirsty in her life. The heat was unbearable. Somebody had to find her. Somebody must come soon.

IX

Jane picked up Letty from the drop-off zone at school. It took thirty minutes just to find her kid, wearing that blazing David Bowie costume no less. Standstill traffic was backed up all the way to the rec center. Parents honked relentlessly at the poor crossing guard. It was almost noon and people were eager to get their essentials done and over with. Schools and businesses were dismissed until Monday morning, or, as Sheriff Baez warned, further notice.

"Jesus wept," Jane said. They were headed to Sugar's Market. (Along with everybody else.) "Wish we could pack up and go. Start a new life somewhere else."

Letty sighed, fogging the passenger window glass. "But Dad's at the cemetery here."

Jane shot a glance at her daughter. "You're right."

"I am?"

"Yes. I don't want to leave Daddy either."

Jane hadn't slept in two days, and she was starting to feel the fatigue. Her long red hair had knots in the braid she'd bobby-pinned to the top of her head. She didn't have the energy to brush it out. She hadn't worn any makeup since Hank died, has barely *washed* her face since Hank died. It had been ages since she last drank, but she looked like she'd gotten loaded the night before with her pale, tired complexion. The thought occurred to her that with four days off she could stop on the way home for some hard liquor. Maybe she'd drink herself to sleep while Letty sat up and watched TV, the two of them locked in that little house waiting for the announcement that the Hillbilly Hammer had been arrested.

"Diner's closing at noon. I managed to sneak out at eleven fifteen." She rested her head on her hand. It was hot. She wondered if Halloween was really today. The days were blending. "Letty, you sure you're alright?"

"I'm fine, Mom."

"I talked to Deputy Dawn when I punched into the timeclock—you know, from last night? She said to expect no less than two patrol vehicles on our street all day. They're not letting their guard down this time," Jane said.

"So, we're safe? We don't gotta worry?"

Jane nodded, as they passed Abe's Liquors. They used to call them state stores when she was a kid. And it was easy then, when she was the age her daughter was now, to buy a few bottles of Jack Daniels and sneak away for the night. The clerks turned a blind eye. She decided *against* drinking through the lockdown.

It crossed Jane's mind to bring something to the Myers family on McClellan, what with Everett's funeral probably getting postponed indefinitely. She prayed to Saint Veronica for comfort. God, they certainly couldn't have an open casket viewing, with that boy's missing head. She wanted to drive up to the church and look at the stained glass. But it was too late in the day. Only a few more hours until lockdown.

"We must be out of our skulls to stay here," Jane said.

"Huh? You're mumbling," Letty said. The blue lightning insignia on her forehead had sweated off, the ink running.

Jane attempted a half-smile, tight-mouthed. "I don't know, baby, I don't know."

Jane held her daughter's hand in her lap the rest of the way to Sugar's Market. All she could think about was the plank wood barricades that kept their home in perpetual darkness. The Hillbilly Hammer had been *in* their house. If only she could talk to Hank about it.

She said, "How about we ask Theo to stay with us the next few days? I think that would be nice."

"Really, Mom?"

"Yes."

Safety in numbers.

They had to wait in a long line for a parking space on

Placerville. The buzzing fury at Sugar's Market was unbelievable. It was worse than the days the town prepped for an impending hurricane. Canned food and supplies flew off the shelves like hotcakes.

"We could use that crossing guard here at the store," Jane said.

Tricia Cross, the radio station lady, reached over Jane's shopping cart for a bag of granny smith apples. "Hey, Janey, you're looking stressed to the max."

"You don't say," Jane said.

"Stay safe, you two."

Stay safe. Jane shivered, and it wasn't from the chill in the produce section. What if they were cooped up for weeks? She gestured for Letty to follow her down the junk food aisle. "What if—"

"What if what?" Letty asked.

"What if we have a Girls' Fort? Potato chips, Halloween candy, popcorn? How does that sound? Don't look at me like that," Jane laughed. "I can have fun, too, Letty Hardin. It's Halloween."

"But what about work?"

"I'm off work until Monday, town's orders."

Letty drew a laugh, grabbing two large bags of assorted

Halloween candy. "Girls' Fort sounds cool. But what about your costume?"

"I'll grab an old bed sheet and cut holes for eyes and be a ghost."

Letty laughed, and it was Jane's favorite sound in the world. If only Hank was here. She'd have felt safer, more loved, stable. They walked down the dairy aisle, loading up on the last gallon of milk on the shelf.

Ben Ashcroft got in line behind them at the checkout. "Afternoon, ladies. Letty, your bike is still in the bushes in front of my trailer. You can pick it up before curfew today if you like."

Jane's face looked worried. "What were you doing in Mr. Ashcroft's yard?"

"Just . . . playing. Nothing, really."

"It's alright, Mrs. Hardin, the girls didn't mean any harm," Ben chuckled. "You can leave the bike at my place as long as you like. Stay safe tonight, ladies."

After a moment waiting in the checkout, Letty looked to her mother. "You mad about it?"

"No, I'm not mad."

Jane was too tired to be mad. She'd had to pinch pennies to get enough groceries for a solid week. Meals were usually whatever she brought home from the diner and bologna sandwiches. Sometimes it was a bowl of cereal. Jane scanned their shopping bags on the way to the car. Did they still have that first aid kit in the bathroom drawer?

"I might not see Bernie and Cam anymore," Letty said.

"Oh?"

"All they care about is trick-or-treating. They don't care about stopping this killer."

Jane took one long look at her daughter as they unloaded groceries into the trunk. "Sounds like you've moved on from Talking Dead Society."

"It's just Bernie and Cam," Letty said. "They're kinda jerks."

"Perhaps you're more mature than they are at this stage in life," Jane said, shutting the trunk. She checked under the car, the backseat, and even under the hood before they got in.

"Let's go see if Theo's home."

X

Tricia informed Ben and Sawyer of an arrest on Sidewinder. A couple kids flying on a Triumph motorcycle, not locals. Because of Tricia's big-shot husband, and the sheer fact the Sugar Bends police department only had three cells and a reception connected to cubicle offices in the building, it was easy to get around. She'd been doing it for years, for the Scarecrows. She knew her way around better than most of the cops that didn't do the booking.

Tricia stirred powdered creamer in a Styrofoam cup of coffee. She didn't expect much from the teens that were arrested, but if they weren't local, maybe it was something to investigate. Sawyer and Tricia stood by the donut display by the water cooler in the booking office. If Fischer came by, they'd chalk it up to Sawyer giving her a ride from Ben Ashcroft's to the market, then back home: almost the truth, except the whole sleeping together and emotional attachment thing.

Fischer walked into the booking office. His gut protruded over his belt. "Sawyer, my man, be glad you got into education. You don't know the delinquents I deal with on a daily basis. Consider your work a cakewalk. Sometimes I wonder why I ever got into law enforcement."

"Things have been rough."

"You can say that again."

"Fish, were those kids drunk driving?" Tricia asked, casually.

Fischer shook his head, sighing. "Sober as a judge. Me and Amy caught them doing ninety on that goddamn motorcycle. Something fuzzy with the engine; that thing roared like I wouldn't believe. Maybe it's going to blow up. I'm not a mechanic. But do you know what they told me when we booked them? Tell 'em, Ginger."

Ginger Ayers giggled over the mail she was sorting at her desk. She'd be one of the few in Sugar Bends to work the entire lockdown. She wore bright pink lipstick. "They said they were in a Chevy and wanted the number for the tow company. They plum forgot."

Tricia and Sawyer saved their concerned glances so Fischer wouldn't see.

"Craziest shit I've heard in a while around here," Fischer said.

"Bizarre," Tricia said.

"Alcohol test came back negative. They seem coherent enough. Dumb as a box of hammers, but what can you do?

They just had to roll into town at a time like this, and frankly, we're going to have to keep them here until Sunday, at the earliest. But if there's a slew of drunks getting their rocks off, we'll have to share cells," Fischer shook his head. He left, headed to the town hall to address haywire residents. After some baiting, Ginger agreed to walk with Tricia and Sawyer into the jail to confront Josiah and Angie.

Ginger offered a glazed donut to Tricia.

"Thanks," Tricia said. She was hungry. "Ginger, those kids, are they in the cell now?"

"Sure are. Jail's empty. Nobody else's booked right now. You have ten minutes, tops, but prepare for five."

When Ginger was out of earshot, Tricia and Sawyer exhaled, exchanging glances. Angie Johnson and Josiah Sullivan. Those weren't names either of them had heard around here, not even in Hounds. The girl's face was red and swollen from crying. She looked battered by life. Tricia couldn't see the boy's face, his head tucked between his knees.

They approached the steel bars.

"Ready for your interrogation?" Sawyer asked. "I'm not a sheriff, and neither is my friend here, Tricia. I'm Sawyer Harris, and this is Tricia Cross. We live here in Sugar Bends."

"Are we going to prison?" Angie asked.

"We just wanted to ask you a few questions. This town has been on high heat lately."

Josiah finally picked his head up from between his knees. His face was beet red. "I just want to know what they did with my truck."

Tricia and Sawyer exchanged glances.

"The sheriff mentioned that," Sawyer said. "You came here on a motorcycle?"

"No. We came here a week ago in a goddamn 1994 Chevy pickup. The thing's beat to shit, so I know nobody didn't take it, but I just put a new battery in her and everything."

"Let me get this straight," Tricia said. "You arrived at Sugar Bends a week ago in a pickup truck. And when you were arrested, the truck was missing, and you were on a bike?"

"Yeah, you heard right," Josiah said, rubbing his hands together. "Pathetic fucking town."

"Be nice to them, Joey," Angie said.

"Nolan Craven," Sawyer said, and Tricia glanced at him, surprised. The kids' faces perked up.

"Yeah, Nolan Craven. It's that guy," Josiah croaked. "I know it is."

Their whole story came out as Tricia listened.

"Where's the headstone now?" Tricia asked.

"I don't know," Josiah said. "Back in that motel room, or wherever he took it to do whatever perverted thing with it."

"This man may not be what you think," Sawyer said. "You're coming with us. You're not safe here. You need to trust me and Tricia. You don't have a choice. Tricia, you distract Ginger and I'll start the car."

Tricia knew exactly where the spare keys were located in the reception booking desk. They piled into the car and drove to the lighthouse on Devil's Hill.

OCTOBER 30

I

T heo passed out from heat exhaustion sometime after the midnight hour, but when she awoke, desert-mouthed and weak, she thought she'd only just dozed off. She knew the sun had set because the entire restroom was cloaked in darkness, and the sunbeams had disappeared from the ceiling. There wasn't any light, but her eyes adjusted just fine. The humidity prickled her skin, but at least it wasn't a wet heat.

"Hello," she said, just to hear something. Her voice was still there. She was still alive and would make it out of here, out of this darkness. Somebody was going to come, sooner or later.

She wondered realistically how long she could stay this way, without food, without water. There was the toilet water. The body could go a long time without food—weeks, if properly hydrated. The thought of drinking toilet water in a public bathroom churned her stomach. She might have to cup her hands into the toilet bowl and drink for hydration. Surely she was losing electrolytes. She wondered when the last time she took a drink of water was. Probably in the work van. Or was it yesterday morning, at Ben's? At the house? Had she drunk anything at Ben's? Coffee dehydrated you. Maybe she'd only had coffee, over twelve hours ago.

The Timber gang defaced this property all the time. Surely, even in town lockdown, they wouldn't be able to keep themselves away. Maybe a trucker needing to relieve themselves would let her out of here. Everett Myers. Maybe they'd have some kind of ceremony for the boy that died out here. Maybe she'd get out of here very soon.

Theo lifted her body forward, off the floor. She concentrated on playing pretend. She pretended she was a child, and she was cold. It was easy to pretend to be cold, picturing a tundra, big and wide. She was in an igloo and her body was freezing, but she was safe, she was fine. She was cold. She wanted ice. She wanted water.

Theo pretended she was up in the Shenandoah mountains on a motorcycle trip with Nancy, like on their honeymoon. They hadn't been young or broke when they legally married in 2015, but they'd pretended to be, riding in a high-altitude Indian summer. She'd just finished paying off the Triumph. Maybe one day she'd feel something other than this unrelenting heat.

Twelve hours passed, thirteen hours. Fourteen. Theo didn't know the time. She sang Patty Griffin, "Don't Let Me Die in

Florida." She used to sing it with Nancy all the time. It was comforting, a little bit. But the singing just made her hotter.

Theo's chest tightened. She felt like she'd just gone running. She looked up at the ceiling, taking in a gulp of air. She just needed cold water. The left side of her head throbbed, and her neck. There wasn't room to stretch her legs unless she went up the wall, which was all she could do.

She focused on the water in the toilet bowl. Another hour of this and—

No, she had to drink water. She had to.

"Fuck," she said, leaning forward. Well, she'd give it one more hour and then take a drink.

II

L isle Baruso floored the gas. The Corvette spun, fluttering a gray cloud of dirt into the air. The other boys screamed. They nearly flew into Pump Gas. It was supposed to be the third burning of the season for Sugar Bends. The sugarcane field was empty of its harvesters, but the acrid smell of smoke hung in the air. Everett's death had rattled the boys. If the town wouldn't give him a funeral, if his own ma and pa wouldn't give him a funeral, the Timber gang would.

Lisle dragged a crowbar along the speed columns in front of Pump Gas. He smashed the dirt-covered glass with the crowbar. The sound was deafening. He pushed his hand through and unlocked it from the inside. Glass sprayed everywhere.

J.T. went behind the counter and grabbed four packs of cigarettes. Marlboros, the expensive ones. "Anybody want anything?"

"Yeah, beer," Lisle said. "Here." He tossed Brent some of what he called "fuckweed," the six-pack spilling from his grasp onto the floor. He tossed a couple more. "Fuck this ugly-ass place."

"Dang, man, what's your problem?" J.T. said.

Lisle kicked a three-tier display of potato chips. It collapsed on impact. He smacked a row of cookies and packaged donuts that went flying. He jumped over the counter and snarled at the cash register, the drawer wide open and empty.

"You didn't say nothing about trashing the place," Brent said. He grabbed a chocolate bar and put it in his shirt pocket.

"The fuck do you care?"

Lisle pulled on the green goblin mask with the black hood, the one that had belonged to Everett. He'd found it back a few days ago when they'd gone looking for him at the campsite, down by Devil's Hill. He'd never told the cops about it. Cops were pigs and investigators would take the shit and give it to Everett's whore mom or something. Lame shit. He'd keep it for himself.

"Come on, kids, grab a mask."

"I don't want to wear a mask," J.T. said. "It's hot as balls out here."

"Pick a mask, J.T., or I'll choose one for you. They're over there."

The plastic Halloween masks were hanging on a display of Halloween candy. They were one dollar. There was a mummy and a frowning pumpkin. J.T. grabbed the mummy and handed the pumpkin off to Brent who flicked the plastic, then put it over his face.

"Smells in here," Brent said.

They trashed more shelves, throwing food to the ground. They opened the freezer door where ice was stored, and left it open, heaving a display of batteries into it so the door wouldn't close. "It'll be water in a few hours," Lisle said.

They ran back to the Corvette and took off down the road near the lumber yard. Beyond the cream- and green-colored stalks, it was too dark to see, even in the early morning light. Usually, the lumber yard operated on a twenty-four-hour basis, but since the stay-at-home order, it was lights out, except the floodlights nearest the highway.

"We should go fuck up that place, too," Lisle said.

"Nah, they're hiring me in the winter," J.T. said. "I don't want to be seen there."

Lisle tossed him a dirty look.

"You're cranky, man," Brent said.

They flew in the Corvette. Lisle popped open a can of beer and chugged, squeezing the aluminum, and tossing it toward the lumber yard.

"It's not kind to litter."

A man suddenly appeared on the passenger side. The boys screamed. Lisle hit the brake as he took his eyes off the road, and the car careened into a guardrail. The man with long black hair and flickering black eyes put his hands on Lisle's arms and a sting of electricity formed, pinging into him. The pulses were small, forward, one right after the other, and then they ceased to be. The boys cried in terror before fainting into death. Nolan Craven removed the green goblin mask from Lisle Baruso's bleeding face and put it over his own, walking off into the lumber yard.

III

Since last night, Tricia and Sawyer had kindly given Angie and Josiah a safe place to crash at the lighthouse. Time was running out, it felt like, and Tricia sure as hell wasn't going to let anything bad happen to these two while her husband stuffed them into a cold cell for trying to escape Nolan Craven. She practiced her well-played part of denial, rehearsing the lies she'd tell Fischer about where the kids went.

The four of them had spoken at length about Nolan, the money that nobody had seen since the glove compartment, Mitch Johnson, the confiscated handgun, the headstone, the Chevy, and the black balloons.

"What do we do if he shows up here?" Angie said. She sat on the couch in the center of the lighthouse's bay room, a blue and white blanket wrapped around her.

"Don't you worry," Sawyer said. "He's not showing up here. We're not what he wants. He wanted the headstone, which he's got. Maybe the worst of this is over."

It was a beautiful balmy day in Sugar Bends, not quite twenty-four hours since the lockdown. The sky was overcast and the laurel oaks flanking Lake Briggs had a sultry tone. Peak autumn in Florida was underway.

"Tricia," Angie said, shyly. "Do you live up here in the lighthouse?"

"I've got enough food in the pantry, I probably could."

"Are you guys married? Me and Joey, we've been married six months."

Tricia was rather tickled at Angie's innocence. She reminded Tricia of her son, Sean, when he was a boy, always clinging to mommy.

The Halloween decorations Tricia had strung around the bay windows were the same ones from when Sean was young. There were paper ghosts hanging above the control station and pumpkins taped to the door. On the bay window was a witch with a paper-brim broom, and some orange and purple tinsel.

Tricia had made the executive decision she was going on the air, whether their small-town government liked it or not. Sugar Bends was scared, and she'd been a comfort to them through hard times. She wasn't about to flip off her light and go home. Not now.

Tricia appreciated that Sawyer didn't try to change her mind. He was a man that let her take charge in the face of strife, whether she was a "real" Scarecrow or not.

"Rain on, Scarecrow," Sawyer said. Angie watched from under the blanket.

Tricia knew she was risking her job, and frankly, when she hit the *On Air* button on the control panel, she almost changed her mind. The radio show had been her life since high school, when she assisted old Blimpy Wagner, the original 101.1 Sugar Bends DJ.

Distinguished listeners of Sugar Bends, this is Tricia Cross on 101.1. It's early for me, and I'm no early bird, but I'm not here for songs tonight. I'm here to warn you about the Hillbilly Hammer.

Tricia's smooth, flirty voice broke, and she trembled, continuing:

My friends, Sugar Bends has a killer out there, and that killer is Nolan Craven. He's responsible for the murders of our friends and family and colleagues, and even our children. So, while your business lights are off and your car is parked in the yard, please pay attention. Lock your doors. If you're smart, you'll quarantine to one dark room in your home and stay quiet until Nolan Craven is captured. He's a dangerous man, and he killed my friends. Listen here: this man will read you. He will hypnotize you. He'll trick you into believing anything.

My friend Sawyer Harris came face-to-face with this man only a few days ago. I'll stay on air to keep you company for as long as you need. As for our communications department? Well, if this is my last show, so be it. If you think you've seen Nolan Craven, a man with long black hair and horseshoe mustache, please contact the police station. You can even contact me here. You know the number.

There's a fog rolling in from Lake Briggs. And we're almost into harvest season. Please—please stay safe. Stay inside and don't open the door for anybody, not even your neighbor. Not even your neighbor.

Sugar Bends was at a standstill. Everything was shut off from the world except the police station where Ginger Ayers ran the hotline and transferred calls to the appropriate somebody. Halloween decorations deflated as the breeze rolled by. When the rain started, the stalks in the cane field rotted in a matter of minutes, and the smell, like earthen rot, permeated the town.

IV

A trick of the light caught Josiah's eye. He got up from the armchair he'd tried napping in and looked out the bay windows at a breeze rushing across the treetops. Nolan Craven was at the bottom of the stairs, shining what looked like a compass in his direction. He flashed it again. Josiah looked over his shoulder to see if anybody else noticed, but Angie was fast asleep. Tricia and Sawyer were sitting at the control panel as Tricia read off texts from residents about thumping or footfalls on the roofs of their homes.

Josiah Sullivan, come here.

Josiah crept out the door. Shades of indigo indicated the rain would be back; a storm was on the horizon. There was a lick of chill in the air. He couldn't help heading out. Something took him over and he needed to see that light again, get to Nolan. The rain started falling, and against his better judgment, Josiah went out. It was too late to turn back.

Nolan handed him a black balloon at the bottom of the stairs. "Here you go, cowboy."

"Where are we going?"

"To the lake."

The soft rain covered their tracks as they took the long, long walk to Lake Briggs. It was several minutes before Josiah realized a coyote trotted alongside them.

V

The restroom was a furnace. Theo's forehead throbbed, in what she could only assume was a dehydration-induced headache, no matter how much repulsive toilet water she drank. The muscles in her legs ached. Cicadas buzzed collectively over bird caws outside—at least she could hear that much. She heard thunder, too, despite the sunbeams splayed on the ceiling. She hoped it would rain and cool down, even a few degrees.

She splashed her arms with toilet water. It was disgusting and lukewarm, but it felt better than a blanket of wet heat. Her lips were chapped. Her stomach ached.

"Fuck," she said, spitting. Her throat hurt, too.

Food hadn't occurred to Theo since yesterday. She hadn't eaten. But the thought of fried eggs, hashbrowns, and bacon came upon her, and she could almost taste it. She got the urge to throw up from the phantom smell.

"I know you can hear me, you son of a bitch," Theo said. "Why don't you man up and bring me some breakfast?"

She paced in the minimal space she had. Moving a little was better than not moving at all.

Her muscles ached something awful. She'd never been

stricken with such hot-to-the-touch anxiety before.

"Nancy, you there?" She didn't expect an answer and didn't receive one.

At some point, she got uncontrollable shakes in her hands. Then her legs trembled, and she forced herself to sit down. Panic washed over her. It was happening: a seizure. She was having a dehydration-induced seizure. Maybe it was heatstroke. She had to breathe through it. She soaked her shirt in the toilet water, wrapping it around her neck so the water dripped down her back and her scalp got wet. She breathed in through her nose, and out through her mouth.

It was just the heat.

Theo drifted in and out of consciousness. Every time she was awakened by her own black and white nightmares, she reminded herself she was breathing, and somebody would come soon.

When she came to, she gazed at the corner window. If only it would shatter. If only it would shatter and the noise from the glass would travel to the street, and somebody heard her shout. But when was the last time she was *capable* of yelling? More air. More air was that way through the corner window. Better, clean air. Anything but this.

Hours came and went, and Theo dreamed about throwing

her steel-toed boot and the glass smashing. She dreamed she climbed over the partition and broke the glass, snaking out the window and running down the street where everybody turned and looked. When Theo awoke, the boot was in her hand.

She threw the boot, missed, and cursed. Were people talking? Were people whispering about her? No, it was a symptom of heat-induced paranoia, she told herself. She was sick. She was dehydrated. She was hungry. But—voices? Maybe they were talking about her. *Who?* she thought. *I don't know.*

"Nancy?" she tried again.

Theo thought about Letty, wondering if she'd found the letter she had left on the kitchen countertop.

VI

Letty watched *Beetlejuice* on the TV in her David Bowie costume, sans the red Converse. She had put in the DVD after turning off *Scream*. *Scream* was funny in parts, but all the fighting off the killer in a drugstore mask wasn't at all like real life. You didn't have a comeback for every dodge of the knife, Letty thought. Everybody asked her how she got away from the Hillbilly Hammer, but she wasn't positive herself. She'd dodged the blow. Ran. Her mom came out of the bedroom. Suddenly, the Hillbilly Hammer was out of sight.

Letty stuffed herself with her favorite candy. She had bowls of candy corn, Snickers, Twix, Skittles, and Dr. Pepper and popcorn on the couch with her. She and her mom's Girls' Fort didn't quite work out. Her mother, engulfed in the darkness of her bedroom with the plywood-covered windows, had fallen asleep and barely stirred the last day and a half. She'd get up to make a cup of tea, take it to bed with her, and then forget about it on the nightstand as she fell back to sleep. Letty knew her mom needed the rest. Plus, eating her weight in junk food while her mother slept wasn't the worst thing in the world.

There was a sliver of her bedroom window that hadn't been covered by plywood, and occasionally, Letty would slip off to her bedroom and pull back the curtain to see if Theo was home. They'd tried getting a hold of Theo, called her cell phone, knocked on her door, but they hadn't seen her since the night the Hillbilly Hammer came. Letty checked in on her mother, too. She peeked her head in and let her eyes adjust to the darkness, just to see her mother's chest rise and fall. She was okay. They were okay. Nobody could get to them.

Letty had fun by herself. After *Beetlejuice*, she decided to watch a VHS copy of *The Lost Boys*, because her mother said it came out when she was in high school—forever ago. The boy on the front cover was super cute. So cute, in fact, that she got distracted, texting pictures of the vampire gang leader to her friends, only half-watching the movie. By the time *The Lost Boys* was over, it was after 11:30 p.m. and pouring rain.

Letty pocketed her pepper spray and an umbrella and trotted next door to Theo's house. Her eyes roved the darkness. All she could see were the patrol cars parked on either side of Loxahatchee Street. Everybody was inside, and the dogs were quiet.

"Hey, Theo?" Letty called. She flipped on every light that wasn't already illuminated. She went down the shotgun hallway to the bedroom. She checked the closet and bathroom. Boy, her mom would have a cow if she knew she'd walked to Theo's house, but she was doing her duty as a member of the Sugar Bends community, and if Letty thought she had any possibility of being a Scarecrow in the future—if they weren't satanic sex maniacs—then she had to start somewhere.

Walking back through the kitchen, Letty found a note on the countertop by the bread box.

Letty,

If you're reading this, it probably means I've been gone too long and there's trouble. Maybe I'm missing. If so, it's Nolan Craven, like we talked about. Go back to your house and call Ben Ashcroft and tell him I'm at The Pits. If I'm not at The Pits, Nolan's taken me somewhere. He's got Nancy and I'm going to get her back. Take care of yourself and your mother.

Theo

Letty's mind raced as she stuffed the letter into her jumpsuit pocket. She texted Bernie and Cameron that it was a life-or-death situation, and they needed to get over here right away.

With the lockdown, it took time to sneak out. Bernie had to wait until her parents went to bed. Cameron showed up first, walking *all* their bikes alongside him in the shadow of the streetlights.

"How did you manage to pull that load?" Letty said, letting him into Theo's house. "Hurry. I don't want anybody to see."

"Jesus Christ, it's wet out there," Cameron sighed. "I almost got caught. I took the long way, went from my street into the woods and then this way—shit, look at my costume."

Cameron's black robes were soaked. He untucked the white mask from his shorts and squeezed the rubber into the kitchen sink. A half hour later, Bernie showed up. Her black hair and Black Panther costume were also soaked.

"Half the houses are boarded up," Bernie said, out of breath. "You'd be surprised how many freaks are sitting out on their porches with shotguns. I've never been so quiet in my life, shit."

Letty bolted the door and showed the letter to her friends, explaining everything. What exactly they'd planned to do, they hadn't calculated, nor had it really mattered in that moment, with the three of them in somebody else's house at midnight, wet from the rain, their town shot to hell.

"I'm not letting Theo do this alone. She'd do it for my dad. I'm gonna do it for Nancy," Letty said.

"What if . . . what if they're dead?" Cameron said.

"Don't say it, because it's not true," Letty said. "Nobody's dead."

"What if Nolan comes after us?" Bernie said. "I mean, what if it's a trap?"

"It's not a trap. Ben Ashcroft is her friend and over my dead body am I going home without a fight. This is our town, too. Don't wig out on me. I need you guys."

"Hey," Bernie said, lightly punching Letty in the shoulder. "Looks like you got your pepper spray back."

"Yeah, I did." She lifted the black canister. "So, no wigging out?"

"Nobody's wigging," Bernie said. "Oh, and I brought something." She heaved a bag of candy corn from a black Jansport over her shoulder.

"Sweet," Cameron said, and they each grabbed a handful, heading outside to their bikes where the rain subsided.

The patrol cars were still parked on either side of Loxahatchee. The cops could've been sleeping for all the friends knew, but they weren't taking any chances. They cut through backyards, walking their bikes until the coast was clear at the end of the street.

"Straight this way," said Letty. "We take Flat Roads west to Placerville and cut through the school drop-off, up to River Cross. Then we take River Cross all the way to The Pits, and we don't stop for nothing. If we get separated, we meet at The Pits."

Bernie shook her head. "At the school drop-off, really?"

"Yeah, cops will see us," Cameron said. "We avoid the school drop-off. We avoid Placerville. We cut through the woods all the way to River Cross. Takes us twice as long but nobody sees us in the dark."

Nobody sees us. Letty liked the sound of that, and she was almost convinced this adventure would be fun, not dangerous, and everything was going to be alright. Out in the woods on their bikes, it felt like summer. Bernie maxed the volume on her phone, putting on an old band her brother listened to: MGMT, "Electric Feel." They could keep track of each other that way, in the woods, in the dark, with only the light of Bernie's phone and the music leading their way.

"Let's do this for Babes Henry!" Letty called, over her shoulder.

"For Babes!" they cheered.

In the woods, "Electric Feel" and the wisp of autumn reunited Talking Dead Society, even for just one night.

"We're coming, Theo," Letty whispered.

OCTOBER 31

I

Theo had another seizure. Her legs ached after, as if she'd hiked a mile with bricks strapped to her thighs. She didn't want to lift her head to see if sunbeams still marked the ceiling. She didn't want to know the time, or how long she'd been here, or how often she felt the sensation to eat. She slept stiffly and dreamlessly after the seizure, only aroused by a snapping branch outside. She shut her eyes, hoping for rescue or a fluttering draft from the opened bathroom door. The promise of another person.

Hot and exhausted, she slid herself to the toilet and drank water. She splashed her face. She heard a snapping branch again, and when she lifted her head, Nancy appeared, curled in the nook of the stall with her.

"Nancy," Theo said, her eyes brimming with tears. "Honey, come here."

Nancy was on her knees, blond hair like a California surf song spilling down her back. Her dark eyes were soft and gentle, and she wore the Mell's Citrus & Nursery apron she'd had on the last day Theo saw her.

"You've come back to me," Theo said.

Theo and Nancy embraced, kissing with unspent affection. Nancy—the same as she ever was, open and vibrant, easy to draw a laugh—was alive, holy shit, she was *alive*.

"I've missed you," Nancy said.

The sound of her voice sent a flutter of agony through Theo. She clasped Nancy's hands in hers, kissed them, and held them to her forehead in a moment of worship. "Where have you been?"

"I've been here, in the utility room with the moaning generator. I knew you'd come for me."

Theo sobbed as Nancy removed her bifocals for her. She wiped the sheen of sweat off Theo's brow and held Theo against her.

"Did he hurt you?" Theo asked.

"It happened so fast, honey, I didn't feel a thing."

"We're going to get the hell out of here," Theo said. "If it's the last thing I ever promise you, I'm going to take you somewhere where this will never happen again. Look at you— you're beautiful, and you're okay. You're okay."

"I'm afraid, sweetheart, that's not possible," Nancy said. She pulled away from Theo, though they were nearly joined at the hip in the small stall, only inches between them, knees touching.

"Why's it not possible?" Theo said. "What are you saying?"

Suddenly, with her wife in her arms, Theo was struck with insatiable fear as a tumultuous static buzzed from her inner ear and down her spine. She'd never heard it so loud before, this vacuous hum erupting from within. The dead. Deadness.

Nancy smiled, a true smile, pretty and bright, wrapped up in twenty-two years of loving her wife.

"Nancy—" Theo started. She understood instinctively. She slipped her bifocals on, a wave of brutal grief washing over her. No. *No.* Her wife wasn't murdered in cold blood. It was impossible.

"It's okay, Theo," Nancy said, still smiling.

"Please," Theo cried. "Please, Nancy, please stay with me. Don't leave me. You were happy with me. You're the only life I have to tend to, to take care of."

Theo became hysterical as Nancy faded. Her eyes flickered black, and her blond hair turned to wisps of corn silk. Her face became wrinkled and black-pored, crone-like. Theo felt herself entering death, like a wormhole opening in deep space. The grooves of her love were shown to her, and she could hear Nancy's heart beating, taking her back in time to the last day she was alive.

II

Nolan appeared as Nancy turned to ash. Nolan waved his hand, and Theo was engulfed in Nancy's memory, her voice, her story.

Theo, my endless joy, I am sorry I didn't tell you sooner. For the last six months, a coyote has watched me. I've seen it in the sugarcane fields on our morning drive to work. While I'm at work I've seen it watching me from the street or hunched between pink camellia hedges in the nursery. I've seen it in the tool shed at home. I'm committed to informing Roberta Quentin and Ben Ashcroft, and the rest of the Scarecrows, if I see the coyote one more time before New Year's Day. I think it is looking for you, not for me. I think that because I don't believe in these dark and strange things that happen in Sugar Bends, not the way you do. I can't process the definition of a ghost, even if I am one now. I almost don't believe what I've witnessed here in Sugar Bends. I don't have it in me. Unfortunately, Theo, by the time I try to tell the Scarecrows about this marble-eyed coyote, I'll be dead. I was murdered on December 28, 2023. Hammer to the head and everything went black. I didn't feel anything. I didn't see him, either. Couldn't pick the man out of a lineup, honey. At first, when I felt myself dying, I thought leaving you would be the worst part, but the worst part is how powerless we are among these greater forces. Nolan has killed me so he can soak up all your grief and live into eternity. You're loud inside and out, Theo. He has the psychic ability to hear the dead too, but nowhere as powerfully as you.

You know the rest. You know what to do. You don't need me to tell you.

You don't need me here like you think you do. Souls can't break and mine is safe with yours until we're together again.

III

alfway through the second playthrough of "Electric Feel," Letty, Bernie, and Cameron peeled out of the woods on their bikes and onto River Cross near the abandoned Bends Mall. A Jeep Wrangler pulled up next to them. It was Ben Ashcroft and Roberta Quentin.

"Look what we have here," Roberta said, hanging her hand out the open window. "When you're right, Ben, you're right."

Ben nodded from the passenger side. "Told you."

"Theo's gonna love this," Roberta said. "There's three of them."

Bernie raised an eyebrow. Her costume was still wet from the rain. "Somebody gonna tell me who the hell you are?"

"Scarecrows," Letty smiled.

Roberta and Ben helped the kids load their bikes onto the back of the Jeep, and everybody piled inside. They drove to the rec center and parked against the athletics building with the engine off. Sheriff Baez spoke to another deputy in the parking lot.

"Shift change," Roberta said. "Tricia said he's on a forty-hour patrol."

Cameron removed his mask. "But what about The Pits?"

"We're headed there," Ben said. "Keep your heads low. Go ahead now, down."

They ducked as another patrol car circled the parking lot. Sheriff Baez got into a squad car with another officer. They didn't seem to notice the Jeep Wrangler.

"Do Scarecrows work for the cops?" Bernie whispered.

Roberta snickered. "Don't bet on it."

Ben informed the kids of the plan. They'd isolate Nolan Craven at the rest stop. Rescue Theo. God willing, rescue Nancy. Call the sheriff. Call Sawyer and Tricia, tell them to put that newlywed couple on a bus and send them home to wherever that was. Throw a party. Simple as that.

Bernie tapped Letty on the knee. "Thought you said this was *our* job to do."

Letty shrugged.

Ben chuckled. "I had a feeling this would happen. Didn't I say that, Roberta?"

"You sure did," Roberta turned on the engine.

When they arrived at The Pits, a residual smell of sulfur was in the air. The palmettos and turned-over picnic tables were still damp from the rain. Roberta parked on the blacktop.

It was Halloween morning. The sun inched its way over the treetops. The Scarecrows forbid the kids to leave the truck.

Letty suspected Ben and Roberta had a firearm with them, based on the clicking sounds in the front seat. She'd seen enough movies to know what a cartridge sounded like, and it made her swallow hard. The Scarecrows left the Wrangler, walking out of sight with Letty, Bernie, and Cameron left in the Wrangler.

"If they don't want our help, why the heck didn't they take us home?" Bernie said. She stuffed her hand inside the bag of candy corn, and Cameron and Letty grabbed some, too.

"Because they'd get caught," Letty said. "And we'd get caught. Do you see anything out there?"

They squinted and leaned into the fogged backseat window, trying to get a look into the patch of darkness up ahead where the tree path met the graffitied courtyard and restrooms.

"Nothin'," Bernie said. "It's too dark."

"It'll be sunup soon," Cameron said. "I'll be grounded for the rest of the year after this."

"Here comes somebody!" Letty said.

"Roberta said if anybody comes, to lay on the horn," Cameron said.

"Wait—wait a minute."

Letty pressed her face against the window. She felt her breath leave her as she saw a man walking up the path, out of the darkness.

"It's my dad!" Letty said. "Daddy!"

Bernie and Cameron exchanged shocked glances, clutching the headrest of the driver's seat in front of them. Letty flung open the passenger door and leapt out. She turned to her friends, tossing the Bowie wig onto the blacktop.

"What the flying hell," Bernie said, but it was too late. She laid on the car horn. "Cam, let's go!"

Bernie and Cameron scrambled out of the Wrangler. Letty dashed through knee-high weeds and crabgrass toward the man wearing powder blue flannel and a worn Bears cap.

"Letty, wait!" Cameron said.

"Don't, Letty, he's not real!" Bernie said.

"Remember what Roberta said! Come back!"

But Daddy looked just like she remembered him. In private, Letty thought of her father as a teddy bear come to life. Oh, and he was. He was the best dad in the whole world. Nobody had a dad like hers. Half the kids she knew didn't even know their dads, or they were deadbeats, like Cam's old man. She didn't just once have a father that she loved, she had a father that loved her.

"Daddy, it's me! Mom and I thought you were gone forever!"

"Hey, firefly, is that you?" Hank Hardin said.

Firefly. She almost forgot he used to call her firefly! He was a heavyset man, tall, with dishwater hair like hers. His apple cheeks were rosy.

Letty ignored her friends and ran into her father's arms for the first time in over two years. "Don't leave me."

"I'm back now."

"It's Nolan Craven!" Bernie shouted, stopping herself from getting too close.

"Open your fucking eyes!" Cameron said.

Letty didn't struggle to understand how her father was alive. Losing him meant losing the sun and summer for all time, and here he was, smelling like smoke and soiled grass from working at the mill.

"Dad, it's really you."

"Yes, firefly, it's really me. Tell me you're real, too," Hank said, holding her at arm's length. His hands were warm like his honey eyes. "You're getting so big."

"I love you," Letty said.

Hank hugged her, and a plume of grief washed over Letty, superseded by pops of electricity in the depths of her eardrum. She'd never heard these sounds before. She felt the electric snaps like boots cascading down a set of stairs, rising all around her. Her belly got hot.

"Dad—" Letty said.

"What, firefly?"

Letty felt his long hair brush against her neck. As she pulled from her father's embrace, she saw the dirty Chippewa boots in the grass on this man, her father. She looked up at his face and he smiled lovingly back at her.

Letty looked up at the nervous sky. It would thunder soon.

"Dad, you still have that feather-braid in your hair, the one I made for you at Girl Scouts." She tenderly stroked the braid.

"That's right, firefly. I've taken such good care of it."

Letty swallowed her trust and longing, glancing down again at the Chippewa boots. "You sure, Dad?"

Hank smiled. He had flecks of corn stalk between the sharp tips of his teeth. "Absolutely. I never take it off."

Bernie scurried out from behind a turned-over picnic table in the grass, just behind Letty and Hank. She threw the pepper spray, and Letty caught the canister midair. She writhed out of the man's arms, pressing the release button as it sprayed Nolan Craven's face.

"Nice try! I never went to Girl Scouts, creep!" Letty said.

A coyote howled from somewhere in the distance. Letty let

go of the release button too quickly, dropping the canister. She felt the mace cloud brush against her face. It felt like fifty miniscule needles penetrating her skin. She screamed as Nolan Craven moaned in pain. She ran into the rest stop, blinded.

IV

*S*ugar Bends, this is Tricia Cross. I'm diving into my twelfth hour here on 101.1. I'm reading your texts and keeping you company on this rainy, hot morning. It's Halloween if you're keeping track. And if you're just waking up with us, we've got a missing young man out there: Josiah John Sullivan, blond hair, blue eyes, Chevron ball cap, about five foot seven and 140 pounds, twenty-one years old. His wife is worried sick. Please, Sugar Bends is in deep enough as it is. Let's stay safe in our homes today.

At 4:04 a.m., I received a text from a resident: our very own Wallace Cato, down in the Tidioute park. He informed me there was somebody on his roof. He could see the shadow of a man outlined on his van, the largest man he'd ever seen. Again—a man on the roof down in the Tidioute area in the middle of the night during lockdown.

At 4:29 a.m., Lexi Reeves of the Cinder Street and Pennecamp block reported three—her words, folks—three men on the roof. Listen to me, Sugar Bends, check your locks right now. Check your windows. Don't wait. If you did it six hours ago, do it again.

Marcelle and Julian Aucoin from Bethel Road reported a man on their roof at 5:10 a.m. Thank you, Marcelle; thank you, Julian, for keeping us informed. Stay safe. Lights on. Keep in touch.

If you had a restful night, text and tell us your secret. I'm not going *anywhere this Halloween. If you're alone, I'm right here with you, baby.*

Here we go. I've just received a text from Gail Ferguson on River Cross and 19th. Good Morning, Gail. Gail tells us that there's a dead coyote on her doorstep. Police have just arrived. Thank you, Gail. Hang in there.

You heard it here, my distinguished listeners, a man on a roof and a dead coyote. The Hillbilly Hammer is still at large. We've got a high of seventy-eight degrees today and a low of fifty-nine. There's a low fog hanging over Lake Briggs, but the sun's up and it looks like it's going to rain again any minute. I'll be back in a few minutes, hold tight.

Tricia pulled the headphones off and sighed, slumping back in her swivel chair. Sawyer caressed her back, his dark eyes a comfort. They kissed tenderly. He hadn't slept either, insisting on keeping watch over the lake, in case Josiah showed up—or the killer.

"I'm worried about her," Tricia said.

They looked somberly at Angie sleeping on the couch, the blanket wrapped around her like a shawl.

"Why that boy left, I'll never know," Sawyer said. "Unless Nolan Craven got a hold of him—maybe put on a disguise, something. This is the darkest this town's ever gotten."

Tricia smiled sheepishly, gazing out the bay windows. Sawyer rested his head on her shoulder.

"I feel like we're safer up here than anywhere else," she said.

"You may be right."

"Even if I do feel like a doomed passenger on a plane running out of fuel."

"Let's watch the lights," Sawyer said. The streetlights turned off in a dreamy, quiet succession as sunrise obscured the fields' smoke.

V

Theo heard a clatter. She laughed, feeling a surge of bile rise in her throat. Somebody was here.

"Theo?" Letty said.

"I told you not to come!" Her voice sounded raspy, cracked. "Hurry. I need fresh air."

Letty got a solid grip on the partition while Theo, too spent for much more than a push, managed to unhitch the door from the swollen caulk. Nolan was more powerful than she could ever feel, or practice to become. "He's coming," Letty said. "Come *on*."

Theo was half-dressed and barefoot, her face like red punch from the heat. She trembled putting on her bifocals. Walking was agony. Her muscles felt like they were clamped together with a medieval instrument. Her thighs were almost numb. The two of them, holding onto each other, stumbled out of the restroom as fresh air washed over Theo. She stumbled, falling to her knees and smiling at the freeing, satisfying feeling. *She could breathe*. Letty helped Theo back to her feet.

"Come on, we gotta go!" Letty said.

Theo and Letty went up the broken steps, pushing open the utility room door, walking right into a tank of propane. They were met with a single fluorescent light shining onto the steel-gray pipes as the generator and water pump chattered in the back of the room.

"The Scarecrows—where are they? Ben, and where's Roberta?" Letty said. "What's that smell?"

"Don't look," Theo said, out of breath. She was ill. She felt her chest tighten when she saw the deteriorating skull spattered in dried gray matter and blood-drenched, unnatural clumps. Theo's mind wandered, remembering the teenage boy that was murdered a few days ago. She slowly drifted around the paint-peeled column, staring like a deer in headlights at the metallic shelf, blood splattered from there to the concrete.

"Letty, I want you to keep your eyes on me, you got it? Don't look at anything else in this room. I'm saving you lots of therapy with Mrs. Sanders in your future. That was funny, right?"

Letty nodded. "Sure."

"Swell. Just keep your eyes closed." Theo seized a shovel. It was better than nothing. She walked back to the utility room door and latched the lock, but it wouldn't hold. "Shit. Did they say which way they were going?"

"I don't know. They said they were coming for you," Letty said.

"Eyes on me."

"I know." Letty sniffled.

"Happy Halloween," said Nolan Craven, striding out of the shadows between the water pump and generator. His face was dominated by his eyes. In his arms, he carried Babes Henry's headstone.

Letty gasped and dove around a unit of copper pipes, hiding behind Theo, who gripped nothing but a shovel.

"What you got there, Nolan?" Theo asked. "Maybe we can carve my wife's name into the other side."

Nolan sat the headstone down on the concrete floor, grinning savagely. The weight of the stone didn't seem to matter to him. "Now that I have you both together, I ask for your attention. I want to make this fair. Which one of you will come with me? You'll have the utmost comforts, borderline immortality, and the gifts of hypnotism and hidden empathy."

"Nobody's going with you," Theo said. "You need a woman and a little girl to spruce up your demonic condition? Why'd you take Nancy? Answer me that."

"Nancy Russo's death hurts me more than it hurts you," Nolan said, with sardonic pleasure. "Unfortunately, if one of you doesn't join me, the murders will continue until I get what I want."

"I'd love to clean your body off this filthy floor," Theo said.

"I've watched you for years, Theo. I didn't expect this radical anger in you. You've certainly kept me energized these last three days; why, having you isolated to that bathroom stall, I could absorb your grief and psychic connection anytime I wanted. I feel rejuvenated just having you near me. You are the fuse."

"Nancy told me you watched us. She got through you, and she came to me. She visited *me* in that bathroom where you caged me like an animal," Theo said. She held the shovel over her head as if in a batting cage. "Turn yourself in and save us all a lot of headache."

Nolan smiled, turning back toward the headstone that he tapped with his pointy fingernail. Theo could see he was going to attack. She could also see there wasn't a way out.

"You're a psychopath," Theo added.

"Born intuitive, burned gifted. Badlands, times five," Nolan said.

His eyes became big black holes as he lifted the headstone and pressed it to his forehead. The room glowed a pulsing shade of gray and white that Theo had never seen before—a shade not of nature. It wasn't as much a color as it was a deluge of black rain, a phenomenon. Suddenly, she smelled smoke.

She smelled firewood. The buzzing commenced.

Theo and Letty threw their hands over their ears, gritting through the pain. Nolan's body vibrated as the black rain poured through him. He looked on the edge of life and death, between conscious electrocution and baptism.

"He's absorbing Babes Henry's grief," Theo yelled, grabbing Letty by the shoulders, and pulled her toward the row of shovels and propane. The fluorescent light flickered. "Don't look!"

Babes Henry was the most grieved person Sugar Bends had ever collectively lost. Nolan took the girl's legacy and turned it into black rain, which washed over him, revving up his hypnotic conjuring.

Theo clenched her jaw, cupping a hand over Letty's shoulder, hoping she'd catch her feelings in a clairvoyant pursuit. *Run*, she wanted to tell her. *Pump your legs as fast as you can.*

The headstone turned to dust. Nolan wiped his hands on his patched jeans and approached Theo and Letty with a hunched, fast stride.

Theo hadn't taken her hand off Letty's shoulder. She hoped she could sense her, hear her, absorb her the way this motherfucker absorbed the grieving. "Leave Letty out of this.

Let her go. I'll come with you."

"Wonderful," Nolan said. "Come here, Theo. Come with me."

Letty snatched the shovel out of Theo's grasp, running head-on into Nolan, who fell backward as the shovel splintered into the soft spaces around his ribcage. Nolan smacked Letty in the neck with his fist. Letty crashed into him, as Theo imagined the specks of circles in her vision as shock poured through her.

As Letty fell and Nolan threw the shovel across the utility room, Theo lurched into him, jamming her finger into his eye sockets and seizing the titanium hammer hanging out of his holster. She struck him in the face. He fell unconscious, moaning and spooling out coagulated blood.

"It's not over," Theo said. "Don't move, Letty."

Nolan's face withered into the wrinkled face of a man born in 1960 and burned in 1988. He was all soot, his hair turning into thin wisps of corn silk. His black eyes, like reversed moons, recalled the black rain. He smelled like firewood.

At that moment, the others—Ben, Roberta, Bernie, and Cameron—burst into the utility room.

"Wrong choice," Nolan managed. A minute later, he was unrecognizable.

VI

Nolan Craven died on that blustery Halloween morning. Letty and Theo watched the whole phenomenon, the nightmare come to life. All that was left was the lingering smell of firewood. The yearlong saga of the Hillbilly Hammer was over. The second lockdown in Sugar Bends's history was lifted the Monday after his death was announced. Nolan Craven was identified as a fifty-five-year-old man, once missing, now deceased. The investigators guessed he'd occupied the utility room at the old rest stop for possibly decades. What he ate, how he survived, was anybody's guess. The only thing they knew for certain was that he was the same Nolan Craven who was burned in the mill fire in 1988.

NOVEMBER 1

I

Theo started from a gentle touch on her hand. An incessant beeping kept rousing her from restful sleep. A blood pressure cuff woke her, too. She lay with a thick bandage wrapped around her forehead.

"Jesus wept, you're awake." Jane was sitting beside her in the hospital bed.

Theo's vision adjusted to the bright fluorescents. She remembered arriving by ambulance, getting pumped full of saline and ketamine. She vaguely recalled the physician telling her she was suffering from arrhythmia induced by severe dehydration and low blood pressure. A round of x-rays while she'd been sedated showed she had a bruised collarbone and two bruised ribs. She'd never felt so weak in her entire life.

"Hi, Jane." She felt stiff, grimacing in pain as she tried to look less formal.

"Don't move a muscle if you can help it. I'll call for the nurse."

Theo forced a smile, wanting Jane to know she was comforted by her presence. Her back hurt like a bitch. She looked down at her legs, cuffed with massaging foam.

"Where's Letty?"

"Letty's fine. Didn't need a single stitch. She's asleep in the waiting room. She didn't want to leave you until you woke up. Smart girl."

Theo noticed her cheekbone aching. Had she lost a tooth in the fight? Maybe. It was the least of her worries. Her moment of grim satisfaction, knowing that motherfucking hillbilly had dropped dead, was followed by a hollow feeling deep inside her. Nancy was dead. Theo witnessed her deadness.

"We got him," Theo murmured.

Jane frowned. Her long, red hair was a messy nest and the bags under her eyes had grayed even more than the last time Theo saw her. "A heartless lunatic, put here for what purpose? I'm praying for her, and for you."

It took Theo a moment to realize Jane's *her* meant Nancy, and not Letty. She was praying for Nancy. A nurse arrived to take Theo's vitals. Her electrolytes were still below normal. They'd increase her saline and release her in the morning.

When the nurse left, Theo remembered the holiday. From her hospital bed, she could see a stuffed black cat dressed up in a bat costume at the nurse's station. There were orange streamers and a grinning pumpkin.

"He said 'Happy Halloween' to me," Theo said.

Jane patted the IV tape. "Don't even give it a second thought."

Theo stifled the urge to ask more questions about what Jane knew about Nolan Craven's death.

"I have something to tell you about Hank." Theo sighed, doing her best to shuffle into a more comfortable position. "His lifeline. That's what I'm calling it from now on, a lifeline. It's the sound I hear when the dead are occupying a space around me. Hank's lifeline is all over you. I wish I'd told you sooner."

Jane put her hand over her mouth in disbelief as she sank back into the rubber-padded visitor's chair.

"Hank's lifeline is the sweetest hum I've ever heard. I know I shouldn't tell you. Getting an antenna for the dead isn't everybody's cup of tea."

Jane's eyes sparkled with tears. "Can he see Letty?"

"He's with her. I can't get near Letty without hearing Hank."

Theo was out of words. She fell asleep. The saline felt like bathwater running through her veins. When she woke up, Jane had taken Letty home, and Sawyer came by. She'd never been so happy to see Sawyer. The charged resentment she'd let build in the last year lifted. Suddenly, being angry didn't seem so important.

"I brought flowers from my kitchen planter—the one Nancy gave me for my birthday. Registration made me leave it downstairs. How are you doing, kid?"

"I've been better."

Sawyer looked at the heart monitor that Theo was hooked up to, the lines and waves on the screen meaningless to him. "You got him."

Theo was quiet for a minute. "Letty did. I just assisted."

"Did anybody tell you where they found Nancy's body?"

She looked at him sharply. "Where?"

Sawyer rubbed his chin. Ever the faithful friend, the man couldn't hide his anguish if his life depended on it. "In that utility room. Nancy was in that room. Her body had been there for a very long time, and, as you know better than I or any of us put together, at this stage, she naturally went into an advanced stage of decay."

"The woman always was skin and bones," Theo snickered.

"I'm so sorry, Theo."

"Me, too. But I got to say goodbye. Maybe I'll feel her again soon."

"I know you will."

"We survived the black rain, Scarecrow," Theo said.

"We sure did."

They sat quietly together for the rest of the afternoon.

NOVEMBER 7

I

NANCY JUDITH RUSSO

WIFE, DAUGHTER, FRIEND, CLOWN, GREEN

THUMB, THE SUN

JANUARY 9, 1983–DECEMBER 28, 2023

Most of Sugar Bends showed up to Nancy Russo's service. Not just friends or former schoolmates or coworkers, but also neighbors and strangers offering their condolences. Theo handwrote a six-page eulogy but didn't read it. She went up to the podium in a simple black romper and leather jacket. She still had a bandage wrapped around her forehead and foam padding her ribcage.

"Whatever flattering things I have to say about Nancy won't even begin to describe my love for her. She was good at everything, and what she wasn't good at, she could fake being good at. She included everybody. She hated my music. She knew how to have a good time, which not everyone is capable of—I wasn't. The absence of Nancy turns love right on its head. Everybody here has had a tremendous loss. I don't think it's going to get better. You don't even have to look on the bright side. You just have to take care of each other, while there's still time."

A viewing wasn't possible, but lowering her into the ground with the Scarecrows, Jane, and Letty by her side was the next best thing. In a last attempt to touch her, to feel Nancy in some way other than in rhythmic hums and eardrum tickles, Theo tossed the hand-carved rocking horse on top of the wooden casket.

"Go. Take care of her, you ugly thing."

After the burial, Theo let the sun warm her face. Clouds merged and blue turned gray as a clap of thunder rolled in. She closed her eyes, counting to three, doing her best to believe she didn't see Nolan Craven staring at her from across the cemetery.

II

Nancy Russo's funeral was the first funeral Letty had been to since her father's. She'd never seen a casket lowered into the ground before. Poor Nancy. Bet she wished she could alert everybody that she was alright, and it had all been one big misunderstanding. It wouldn't be the weirdest thing to happen in Sugar Bends. Letty, Bernie, and Cameron, in their best clothing, stood around the fresh grave with long faces. They'd return to school on Monday, and, frankly, it wasn't the worst thing. They'd been pumped for details about Nolan Craven by everyone from detectives to the local news, neighbors, family, and classmates. Half of the time, they weren't even sure of what they'd seen on that blustery morning.

"I'm going to miss Nancy," Letty said.

"Me too," said Cameron. "Hey, maybe she and Babes will give you a sign from beyond, the one you've been practicing for."

Letty's hair, now down to her hips, blew in the wind. "I think Babes Henry has more important things to do where she is."

She bent down to run her fingers along the dates etched in

the stonework. She wondered how often Theo would return here, thinking of the way she still intended to play around her father, buried not far from this row of graves.

"We got something to say," Bernie said.

"We do?"

Bernie nudged Cameron. "Oh, right. We do."

"We believe you about Talking Dead Society, about the dead talking, and all that stuff. And we think it's pretty cool and we're sorry for being dicks."

Letty smiled. She looked off at her mother, standing next to Theo underneath a laurel whose green branches blew in the increasing wind. She fingered the pepper spray canister in her pocket.

She said, "I'm not mad about it. I don't know. Maybe I won't practice right now. I've got too much else to think about."

"You do?" Cameron asked.

"Well, Nolan Craven's a loser creep. He thought he could take away all this good stuff from us, but he didn't, not everything. Not the most important thing."

"Friendship?" Bernie said, putting her good arm around Letty, her black curls and Letty's dishwater strands mingling between them.

"Yeah," Letty smiled. "And memories with my dad."

III

A
ngie checked the trunk of Tricia's truck to make sure she had everything, which wasn't much to begin with. She had a duffel bag now, which Roberta eagerly packed for her, filled with clothes, toiletries, snacks for the road, and a checking account receipt for fifty thousand dollars (the cash, discovered by Ben in a sack on the side of the road where the Ramblin' Man had gotten them). Not even the lousy deputy, who still insisted on ticketing Angie for speeding, knew about the fifty grand. Whatever happened to the Chevy, only Nolan Craven knew.

Sawyer and Tricia approached Angie to see her off. In public, they stood three feet apart, not touching.

"Hey, I just want to thank you guys for everything," Angie said, bashfully. "Any word on Joey?"

"No, honey, I'm afraid not," Tricia said, crossing her arms. "Even if you're leaving, we're not going to stop looking."

Angie shook her head sadly. "Nolan Craven must've taken him. Did they search the lake yet?"

"They have," Sawyer said.

Her departure fell on the first day since Josiah's disappearance at the lighthouse that Angie was functional. She thought, secretly, that perhaps Josiah had actually left her, in the same way his father had left him when he was in diapers and his mama was pregnant with another one. Men did that, and sometimes it would take you by surprise. She knew that from what other women told her, what her instincts told her. Josiah was no saint. But she missed him, and hoped he'd come home to her, and they could have a baby.

"You've got your plane ticket?" Sawyer asked.

Angie nodded. "I ain't never been on a plane before."

Tricia smiled. "Tennessee bound. It won't be more than a couple hours. Your father's picking you up at the airport?"

"Sure is."

"I bet he misses you."

"You bet he does."

Sawyer put a fatherly hand on Angie's shoulder. "You're always welcome in Sugar Bends, Angie. I'm sorry we couldn't help you more."

The sky turned navy, turbulent. The air smelled wet. It would rain any minute. Tricia drove Angie to the airport near Tallahassee. The whole way, Angie looked at the receipt for the fifty grand, wondering what to do with it. The money was hers. She wasn't an outlaw no more. She was taking that flight to Tennessee, but she definitely wasn't on her way home.

NOVEMBER 9

A cold front was coming, and Jane hoped it would stay long enough that she could relish in the promise of the forthcoming new year. She'd spent the morning unboarding the house, collecting nails in a mason jar for the tool shed. It took her three hours, and by the end, the blue cracker house looked like a home again. She peeled the aluminum off the windows and opened the curtains. Natural sunlight filled their space for the first time in ages.

Jane noticed how the damp stench that rolled across town after the last sugarcane burn evaporated earlier than usual. The crisp temperature had sure done Sugar Bends a favor. The last burn was November 3 and the next one wouldn't be until mid-May. For now, she could smell jasmine, pine, and citrus trees again.

-Jane wiped her dirty hands on a rag. She sat on the porch, her feet on the broken step. She listened. She listened this time, instead of praying. She hoped for Hank to touch her, speak to her. When nothing came, she smiled, watching their daughter pull up to the sidewalk on her bike, home at last, the world carrying on.

NOVEMBER 10

T heo checked into a different motel than the one the night before last, pepped on coffee. She was outside Pennington County, up in South Dakota in the Badlands. She'd gotten here on the Triumph, listening to Dusty Springfield, and planned to stay awhile, at least until the first snow. She'd been up at dawn watching bighorn sheep roam in a juniper forest. She rode on into the desert with the canyons shooting up either side of her. The only other humans she saw were the Lakota locals. Most of the prairies and trails were getting ready to shut down, or they'd already closed for the season. She desperately needed the isolation, just her and the mountain fresh air. The frost cooled the burning memory of what happened back in Sugar Bends, spilling out of her and into the slash valley she rode against.

"That's a nice hog you got out there, ma'am." The motel clerk gestured to the parking lot.

"Thanks," Theo said. "Think it's gonna snow?"

The young man shrugged. "Maybe. But it's pretty warm for snow. Don't forget your key. Checkout's at eleven."

But Theo would be late for that. The morning was too good to miss, the views knocking the wind right out of her. She wore steel-toed boots to sidestep cactus. It was probably too cold for snakes, even rattlers. Somewhere among the rocky canyons, she pulled off the road. There were bison in the distance. She took off her helmet.

Her phone vibrated: Sawyer was calling her. It was probably urgent, but she couldn't bring herself to answer. She turned her phone off. She revved the engine.

Theo rode north of the Medicine Root, her braids blowing on the looping desert highway. God, it was freezing. But it was perfect.

"Isn't this fun?" Theo said, looking over her shoulder.

For an instant, Nancy was there, smiling brightly and holding Theo's waist as they rode into the starry Badlands, the wind licking their hair. When Theo turned back to the road, she knew Nancy was gone. She gunned the engine just the same, chasing the lasting sense of their infinite love like a gleaming highway into her soul.

FUTURE - TIME UNKNOWN

olan Craven, in the form of a ghost, of a bad man still throttled on grief and evil walked for miles with Josiah Sullivan next to him. They weren't in Florida anymore. They were much further up in the country, deep in the canyons where you could drive for miles and not see another person.

Josiah carried a black balloon so Nolan could see him. Josiah heard a motorcycle in his ear constantly. It never quit. It made his head ache. That hog had rumbled for so long, he forgot who it belonged to or why it was happening at all. Nolan hummed, and when he spoke to Josiah, his voice was toneless. Josiah couldn't remember their relationship's origins. He couldn't remember anything, not even Angie. He was Nolan's fuse, for now. He was Badlands, times five. He was infinite darkness, in rock and stone, and when they arrived at the next small town, Nolan promised Josiah he'd let him remember his old life. The smell of firewood was all around.

Acknowledgments

I'd like to give a million thanks to Ravven White and Curious Corvid for their intrepid trust and dedication to their authors and love for the story craft. My second book has a forever home. Thanks to editor, Maddy Leary, for making *Black Rain Season* the best it could be. It was a pleasure working with you. Thanks to editor, Anna Corbeaux, for catching everything I couldn't see. Thanks to Matthew Revert for nailing the book cover with your art. Thanks to C. R. Foster for being this novel's earliest reader and your steadfast friendship. Thanks to Serdar, for everything. Here's to all the women and queer horror writers, filmmakers, and artists that have come before me, are here inspiring me today, and will lead this genre in the future. Thanks, most of all, to the readers.

About The Author

Kayli Scholz is the author of *Saint Grit*, *Yeehaw Junction*, and various short stories. She loves all things horror, cryptids, and her cats. She writes from the wilds of Florida.

Find her online at kaylischolz.com.

Printed in the USA
CPSIA information can be obtained
at www.ICGtesting.com
LVHW021256170924
791310LV00001B/24

9 781959 860440